Smoking

HOT

Sex Stories

Volume 3

Darren G. Burton

Humping Iron

D erek arrived at the gym not feeling particularly motivated. The time was nudging towards ten o'clock at night and his body clock was used to working out in the early afternoon. It would be tough, but he really didn't want to miss a workout just now. He was determined to get into prime shape over the next few months and that required being dedicated and putting the effort in.

"Lucky this gym's open twenty four hours," he mumbled to himself and swiped his card to gain entry.

Once inside he paused to glance around and discovered there was only one other person in there. It was a guy around mid-forties and he was currently pushing out some slow reps on the bench press.

Derek hopped onto a treadmill for a warm-up and set it at a moderate speed. The guy on bench press grunted out a final rep, got up, snatched up a barbell and commenced doing some curls. He groaned loudly with each repetition, a sound that started to grate on Derek's nerves a little. That didn't normally bother him.

Must be the late hour, he decided and trained his focus on the little TV screen in front of him.

Music was playing through the gym's sound system. The same bunch of songs were repeated every other day and Derek

3

had learned to tune out to it, rather than enjoy it and use the beat as a workout motivator. Maybe he would start bringing his headphones and listening to his own music selection through his smartphone.

Five minutes later he got off the treadmill and decided it was time to get into some weights. He performed a few quick stretches, then placed his towel on the seat of the lat pull-down machine and did a light set of reps to loosen up. The guy who had been doing curls appeared to have finished his workout and went into one of the shower rooms to wash off the sweat. By the time Derek had finished three more sets and was moving on to the next piece of equipment, the man stepped from the shower in fresh clothes and exited the gym, leaving Derek all alone in the place. He didn't mind. He could take his time. No issues with having to wait to use equipment or holding anyone up.

A Robbie Williams song came on the stereo. He'd heard it at least a hundred times by now, but he didn't mind this track. He used it to motivate him to blast out several quick sets of tricep curls before moving onto biceps. Just as the song was fading to an end he heard someone enter the gym. Derek dropped the weight stack and glanced towards the front door. He smiled when he saw who it was.

Penny was the gym's manager. She usually worked during the day, so Derek wasn't sure why she would be here at this late hour. She was a petite blue-eyed blonde and, whether she was working out or not, always wore tight-fitting training gear.

Tonight she had on a red singlet top that exhibited the bulge of her generous breasts quite nicely. Little white Lycra shorts hugged her hips and buttocks like a second skin. Derek was sure she never wore any underwear under those shorts, as he could always make out the outline of her pouch where the seam split her pussy lips apart. She first went to the desk that ran along the front wall and checked something on one of the computers. After she was finished there she headed towards a locked room that was accessible only to staff. When she saw Derek she smiled brightly.

"Hi, Derek. You're working out late today."

"I know. I couldn't get here earlier due to work commitments. Speaking of which. How come you're in here so late?"

She shrugged. "Just had a couple of things to tidy up."

Penny was obviously wearing no bra under that top because her pert nipples were threatening to bore holes through the material. Derek had to force his gaze back to her pretty face, but it was too late. The slight smirk curling her lips told him she'd noticed him perving on her.

"You been here long?" she said.

"Nah. Haven't even worked up a sweat yet."

"Good," she answered rather strangely and disappeared into the staff room, closing the door behind her.

Something about being alone in this gym at night with sexy Penny was starting to make his blood boil. The hormones were

5

racing through his veins and making him feel a little light-headed. A few months ago he'd gone on a holiday to Thailand, where he'd taken great pleasure in frequenting all the Go-Go bars, shagging himself silly every single night. It had been a constant conveyor belt of little Thai's hotties coming and going from his hotel room. But since being back home a sexual drought had set in. It was a hell of a lot tougher getting laid here than it was in Thailand, hence he hadn't had sex since he'd been back. And that had been a little over two months now.

Times were lean and he was hanging out for a bit of pussy action.

Penny emerged from the staff room, glanced his way, then walked casually towards the front door. Derek thought she might be leaving, and was quite surprised when she paused at the door and locked it, effectively barring anyone else from entering the gym. Again she went to the computers, played around for a bit, then came over and sat on a piece of exercise equipment beside the machine where Derek was currently doing some leg presses. Penny propped a foot up onto the cushion and sat with her legs parted. Derek stole a furtive glance at her crotch and swore he could see a tiny patch of wetness where her opening was beneath the white Lycra. Immediately he felt his cock stir as he tried to concentrate on pushing out the last few reps. She watched him finish his set. He couldn't stop thinking about her damp crotch. Was she feeling horny? Should he take a punt and put the hard word on her?

"Your legs are looking really good," Penny commented as he stood up. "Looking really muscly." She smiled a little lewdly then and added, "Sometimes working in this place gets me a little turned on, seeing all this hot flesh every day." She smiled at him again and moved off towards the staff room once more, leaving Derek standing there feeling dumbfounded.

Had that been an invitation? he wondered. Was she dropping hints that she needed a good fucking? By him?

If he came onto her and he was wrong, he risked getting kicked out of the gym.

"Who gives a shit," he whispered and moved off to hunt her down. Hell, he could always join a different gym.

Suddenly the lights and music went off and the place was plunged into darkness. Derek walked headlong into a machine, banging his knee into a metal bar. He stood there rubbing the sting from his injury and waited for his eyes to adjust to the gloom. Some dull streetlight was coming in through the windows and soon he could make out the shadowy figures of the equipment.

What had happened? Had there been a power failure?

He sensed the presence behind him a moment before he felt two soft, feminine hands caress the cheeks of his butt. He knew it was Penny because he smelt the familiar scent of her perfume. She always wore the same one.

"I don't want anyone to see what we're doing in here?" she hissed in his ear.

"And what *are* we doing in here?" he managed to say. All he could think about was fucking her senseless and the throbbing in his shorts was begging him to do just that.

"I told you, I'm feeling horny." Her arms were wrapping around him from behind now, her athletic little body pressed hard up against his. She started nibbling on his neck, her lips soft and moist, her breath hot against his skin. "You'd like to fuck me, wouldn't you, Derek?"

"*Like* is an understatement," he replied and spun around, planting a wet kiss firmly on her mouth. Her tongue was on the move and he reciprocated. She ground her crotch against his hard-on, making herself gasp in the process. Penny tongued him furiously now as he seized her firm little ass and helped her rub herself up against him.

He lifted her singlet top and roughly ripped it off over her head. She was just as quick to strip him of his shirt, exposing his muscular torso. She rubbed her tits against his chest and he felt her stiff nipples touching his. With no inhibition whatsoever, she grabbed a handful of his cock through the material of his shorts and gave it a hard squeeze.

"That feels big," she whispered hoarsely. "And so fucking hard. That's exactly what I need."

Derek said nothing. He just stood there as the gym manager dropped down on her haunches, expertly tugging his shorts down his legs at the same time. His raging cock sprang out like a serpent about to strike. It hung there, throbbing with raw energy.

In the darkness he saw Penny lick her lips as she eyed his dick. Ever so slowly she moved her mouth closer to it until she was kissing the head. Her tongue flicked out, ran several quick circles around the taut skin before she plunged her mouth down his shaft, swallowing two thirds of his length in one hungry gulp.

"Fuck!" he managed to say.

He put a hand on the back of her head and pushed, urging her to deep-throat his entire length. Penny gagged and withdrew. She spat him out and said, "It's too big to swallow it all."

Derek loved that comment. He let her do her own thing while he just stood there and lapped up the attention.

Her hot, wet tongue was all over his balls now, licking them as if they were delicious sweets. She sucked one into her mouth, used her hand to squeeze them together, then sucked on both at the same time.

Was he dreaming? Was this really happening? He'd been coming to this gym on and off for several years and nothing like this had ever happened before. Penny had been the manager for most of that time and, whilst she was always friendly to him, there had never been any indication she had the hots for him.

Time and chance, he decided and watched her head bob up and down in the darkness. There were cameras in the gym, but they wouldn't be able to record anything that was happening in this gloom.

"That feels fucking great," Derek told her and she sucked him even harder in response to his words. "Take it in deep again." She did as he requested and swallowed as much of him as she could manage.

"I hope you plan to return the favour," she said after withdrawing.

Penny got up and whipped off those tight little shorts. Derek had been right. She hadn't been wearing any underwear. She sat on the cushioned seat of some nearby gym equipment and waited with her legs crossed. Derek got the hint and shed the remainder of his clothes. As he moved in close to her she opened her legs up to expose a pussy that was completely waxed smooth. He cupped her face in his hands and kissed her again. Penny's hand searched out his cock and she stroked it while they tongued. Derek kissed down her throat and onto her chest, where he spent a few moments feasting on her luscious boobs. She sighed as he nibbled on her nipples, running her hands through his hair and clawing at his scalp with her long nails.

"Taste my pussy," she said in such a sultry voice that there was no way he could resist a moment longer. He knelt down between her parted thighs and buried his face in her hot, wet cunt. "Oh, yeah!" she gasped when his tongue slithered into her wet tunnel.

She was soaked and obviously as horny as he was. Derek bit into her hardened clit, sucked it, ran his tongue firmly all over it. All the while Penny massaged his scalp with her fingertips and howled like a cat on heat. As much as he was enjoying eating her sweet pussy, he didn't know if he could do it for long. He was so desperate to fuck her and fuck her hard, he was using every ounce of willpower he had just to hold off a little longer and keep pleasuring her with his mouth.

"You're good at that," Penny said in way of encouragement.

Derek responded and sucked on her cunt, drawing her lips into his mouth and extracting her nectar as if her were dining on a juicy piece of fruit. His cock was throbbing out of control, nagging him to slip it into her luscious hole.

Just another minute or two, he told himself.

In the end lust got the better of Penny and she said, "Fuck me."

Derek wasted no time in entering her and burying his shaft deep inside her wet passage. They both gasped on entry and he soon got into a steady rhythm, gradually building up the tempo until he was literally pounding her into the seat. Penny grasped her ankles with her hands, pulling her feet back behind her head and really opening up her pussy so he could probe it with deep, hard strokes. His balls slapped against the cheeks of her ass as he gave it to her and he had her panting out of control.

He smiled in the darkness.

"This is so much better than any gym workout," he said.

Penny giggled. "I should hope so." She giggled again. "No better exercise than good, hard sex in my opinion."

He couldn't argue with that.

Derek concentrated on bringing his sexy lover to a climax then, drilling her deeply with aggressive strokes until she was squirming around in total ecstasy. As her orgasm waned he slowed his pace and gradually came to a stop. They both rested for a minute so they could get their breath back, then Penny announced that her favorite position was reverse cowgirl and that they should try that now.

Derek wasn't going to argue with that suggestion, either.

The pair switched positions. Penny straddled him, held his cock upright and lowered herself onto it, impaling her hungry pussy with his rigid length. Juice flooded her cunt and seeped out through her opening.

"You're so tight," he said from behind her. He ran his hands over her immaculate ass and decided it had to be the prefect butt, in both size and shape. He gripped her hips as she started to rise and fall, moving slowly and sensually. Occasionally Derek let loose with a flurry of thrusts from below, then would relax again and just let her do the work at her own pace.

She certainly knew how to ride a cock and it became pretty obvious why this was her favorite position. Penny came within minutes. She not only had an orgasm: She squirted! That was the ultimate turn on. Still she didn't stop there. She kept on bouncing up and down, harder and faster until she climaxed a second time, quickly followed by a third.

Hell, this girl could come!

"Fuck it," he told her and hammered into her with some powerful thrusts of his own. "I want you to come again."

"Don't worry," she panted and leaned well forward. "I will."

Even though there wasn't much light in the place, Derek still had a fairly clear view of her pussy sliding up and down his shaft. His cock was glimmering with her wetness as she fucked it. He felt like he was getting close to a climax himself, but wanted to hold back until she'd had one more herself.

It was good for the ego.

Penny slammed herself down onto his dick until she came once more. This orgasm lasted half as long as the others and was nowhere near as intense. She stopped thrusting and just sat there a moment to catch her breath.

Suddenly she sprang to her feet, spun around and dropped to her knees before him. She took a firm hold of his cock and licked the head like an ice cream. She smiled up at him, her teeth white in the darkness.

"It's time to make you come," she said and took his cock deep down her throat.

Using one hand to pump the shaft and her other to stimulate his balls, Penny worked away on the head with her lips and tongue, and Derek knew she'd be able to make him explode no problem at all. Her hand went faster and faster while her mouth sucked harder and harder. It was the kind of blowjob one saw in pornos. It was perfect.

Tingles surged through his loins and he unloaded into her mouth. Penny groaned with pleasure as she gratefully swallowed his seed, extracting every single drop of cum from his dick. He finished with a satisfied grunt and she finished by happily smacking her lips.

"Bet you weren't expecting this when you came to the gym tonight," she said after a while.

Derek grinned. "I like surprises."

Jenna and Jade Ride a Cowboy

T he sun disappeared behind a cloud as Jenna and Jade made their way through the woods. Each had a backpack slung over their shoulders, with food and drink, towels and a picnic blanket. They were heading towards a creek which should be somewhere up ahead and not too far away now.

"I'm starting to sweat," Jade grumbled as she pushed past a low-lying branch.

"Ow!" Jenna groaned when the branch swung back and slapped her across the face.

"Sorry," Jade offered as she forged ahead.

The pair broke free of the dense forest into a field of long grass. Just the odd tree dotted the landscape here. About two hundred yards up ahead the forest grew thick again.

Jade veered to the left and Jenna followed.

"I hope there're no snakes in here," Jenna said, warily eyeing the ground around her feet.

Jade said, "I've never seen any."

"Come here often, do you?"

"Every now and then. I used to come out here with Ben a fair bit when we were together. Had some really fun times out here, actually." She chuckled at the fond memories.

"Are we getting close to the creek?" Jenna wanted to know.

"Just up here."

Soon Jenna could hear the soothing symphony of water running over river stones. The long grass tailed down into a much shorter and greener lawn beside the water. Sunlight glinted off the creek as the water made its way to the left. Jade stopped just on the edge of the woods and dumped her pack. Jenna stood there a moment taking in the scenery. A trail led through the forest and she could make out distinct patterns in the dirt from horse's hooves.

Jade was already spreading the picnic blanket out on the grass. Jenna dropped to her knees on the blanket and started unpacking food and drinks from her own pack. Once the girls were comfortable they opened a can of Coke each and began nibbling on some cheese and crackers.

"Maybe we should have brought some wine?" Jenna said as she stared at the rhythmic motion of the stream before her.

"Alcohol in daytime just makes me sleepy," Jade confessed. "I'm strictly a night time drinker."

"I prefer that too," said Jenna before she took a sip of Coke. It was a tad warm, but bearable. She handed her friend a chicken sandwich wrapped in foil, then unwrapped one for herself. After biting into it she washed it down with more Coke.

"This is perfect weather," Jade commented between bites on her sandwich. "Nice and sunny, but not too hot."

"Perfect weather to get naked and get a tan."

Jade grinned. "That's exactly what I was thinking."

When they'd both had their fill of food, the pair stripped completely nude and spread themselves out on the blanket facing the sun. It tingled on Jenna's skin and a light breeze caressed her flesh. She felt shivers of pleasure coarse through her and she started to feel a bit randy.

"Are you thinking what I'm thinking?" she said to Jade.

"I don't know, Babe. What are you thinking?"

"That I'm feeling a little bit horny," Jenna admitted.

Her interest piqued, Jade propped herself up on an elbow and faced Jenna. "You wanna make love out here?"

Jenna shrugged. "Why not? Beats doing it in bed all the time."

"And it'd create new sexual memories here that don't include Ben."

The girls had been friends for about a year and, since Jade split with Ben four months ago, she and Jenna had started up a casual sexual relationship to add a new and titillating dimension to that friendship.

With her pussy lubricating at a rapid rate, Jenna stripped out of her top, shorts and panties and spread herself out on the blanket, her legs slightly apart. She then watched with keen eyes as her girlfriend shed her clothes, exposing a luscious naked form that was free of fat and had curves in all the right places. Her generous breasts hung tantalizingly close to Jenna's face as the other woman leaned over her.

Jade licked her lips and said, "I want to go down on you."

Jenna grinned. "Do it then." And she proceeded to open her legs wide.

Jade took her time positioning herself between Jenna's thighs. Once down low she lightly flicked her tongue all over Jenna's engorged clitoris, sending shivers of delight through her body. More juice flooded her cunt and she couldn't wait to feel Jade's talented tongue probing her desperate passage.

"Tongue-fuck me," Jenna urged her lover.

With a grin, Jade plunged her tongue deep inside her, then proceeded to suck hard on her labia. Jenna quivered on the blanket and let out a soft squeal of pleasure. She then went into a series of urgent pants as Jade thrust her tongue in and out in a rapid motion that was making Jenna's head spin with desire and hormone overload.

"Oh...God!" she said and bucked her hips, driving her cunt hard against Jade's face. "Fucking tongue me!"

And tongue her Jade did, thrusting inside her wet passage with all the hunger and vigor of a starving woman. Jenna felt the tingles inside her cunt quickly intensify. She was positively throbbing with pent up desire and knew she was getting close to an explosion. Any second now and she would be creaming all over Jade's pretty little face.

Still she rocked her hips back and forth, adding a level of friction to the mix that was bound to make her climax. Her muscles seized up just as her tension reached a crescendo. She came with much relief and saw stars dance before her eyes as the orgasm made her head spin once more. Jenna couldn't help but scream her lungs out as she was overcome with total euphoria. When she was done she lay there gasping like a fish out of water.

"I think that was the best orgasm I've ever had on your tongue," she said eventually and broke into a grin.

Jade returned her smile and said, "That must mean I'm getting better at pleasing you."

"You always please me."

Right then they both fell silent and glanced towards the path leading through the nearby forest. They'd both detected the sound at the same time, the unmistakable clip-clop of horse's hooves on dirt. From the shadows of the woods a man on horseback appeared. When he spied the two naked females sprawled out on the picnic blanket, he brought his horse to a halt and sat there grinning down at them, his eyes hidden behind dark sunglasses.

The man wasn't really dressed like a typical cowboy. He wore no hat, nor boots. His feet were clad in blue and white running shoes. The man had on jeans and a red muscle top. Through the arm holes protruded muscular arms with bulging biceps. Jenna found herself licking her lips, and when she glanced at Jade, she saw her friend was doing the same. She knew then that they were both having the exact same thought.

Let's do the cowboy!

The man climbed down from his horse and secured the reins

to the branches of a plant.

"Wanna join us?" Jade asked the question that both ladies were deliriously thinking.

He smiled a handsome smile. "I was hoping you might say that."

He kicked off his shoes, took off his sunnies and knelt down on the picnic blanket. "I'm Dylan, by the way."

After the girls had said their names, no more words of introduction were spoken. From that point on it was all action. Immediately Jade went to work undoing Dylan's jeans while Jenna helped him out of his shirt. Once his muscular torso was fully exposed, she took great pleasure in running her eager hands all over his skin. She kissed the cowboy on the lips, and as she did so she heard a sucking sound coming from lower down. Peeling her lips away from Dylan's, Jenna saw Jade had a mouth full of long, thick, hard cock.

Dylan let out a loud groan as his cock slid deep down Jade's hungry throat. Jenna watched her girlfriend for a moment, then took pleasure in sucking on the cowboy's small nipples. While she did this she cupped one of his very firm butt cheeks in her right hand and used the fingers of her left hand to massage the bobbing head of Jade.

"Kiss me," Dylan ordered Jenna and she readily responded.

The moment his tongue slipped into her open mouth she felt her aching pussy squirm. She tongued him back, quite furiously, thrusting her tongue deep down his throat as his cock repeatedly disappeared down Jade's throat. Jade was quite vocal in her cock sucking, making loud slurping sounds and moaning with pleasure as she enjoyed the sensation of his throbbing prick between her lips.

Jenna ceased kissing Dylan and dropped to her knees, wanting to taste that magnificent tool. She wrestled the cock from Jade's mouth and wrapped her own moist lips around it. As she took several inches into her mouth she felt it throb as it slid down her throat. Jenna sucked hard while her girlfriend got down really low and flicked her tongue all over Dylan's shaven sack.

"Fuck!" he groaned and shuddered from the intensity of Jenna's sucking. "Suck my balls," he told Jade, and she happily complied.

The girls alternated between sucking cock and sucking testicles. Jenna was loving every second of their felatio. As much as she enjoyed making love to Jade, she sure missed having a lovely hard cock in the mix. Maybe they could make having a threesome a regular event? Judging by Jade's enthusiasm, she'd been missing a male member equally as much as Jenna had.

When it was Jenna's turn again to take Dylan down her throat, Dylan gripped her head in his hands and aggressively thrust his cock in and out of her mouth. Jade clamped a hand around the base of his shaft and jerked him off as he fucked Jenna's lips.

"I need to ride this cock," Jade said and got to her feet, where she pushed Dylan down onto the blanket. When he'd spread himself out prone, she squatted above his cock reverse cowgirl style and raised it upright with her hand. There she paused with the glistening head just touching her opening. She grinned at Jenna, who was eagerly waiting to watch the entry. "This is gonna feel so fucking good." With those words she plunged down Dylan's long length and squealed as her cunt was completely impaled on Dylan's meaty cock.

Jenna couldn't help but grin from ear to ear as she watched her partner fucking a nice big dick. She loved the way its girth was making Jade's cunt lips stretch wide apart. Every time she rose up his shank her pussy left behind a fresh sheen of luscious juice. Jade was soaking wet.

"Come sit on my face," Dylan suggested. "I wanna drink from your horny little pussy."

Anticipation ending tingles of excitement through her, Jenna planted her puss onto Dylan's waiting mouth. Immediately his tongue snaked inside her cunt, causing her to gasp and sending a fresh river of juice into her passage.

As Dylan tongued her cunt, Jenna reached around Jade's bouncing body and grabbed her breasts in her hands. Her nipples were stiff and as hard as her clit. They felt magnificent in Jenna's palms.

"My God, this cock feels good!" Jade suddenly exclaimed. "I'm getting close to coming already."

"Do it, Babe," Jenna urged her girlfriend. "Come all over his beautiful dick."

She continued to grasp Jade's tits as the other girl fucked Dylan furiously on her way to orgasmic glory. Jenna, meanwhile, was positively drooling over the feel of the cowboy's mouth lavishing her cunt with licks and kisses and tender bites. She could feel her juices flooding into Dylan's mouth and every so often he would suck them down his throat.

Jade came with an ear-piercing scream as her body went into a series of pleasurable shudders. Jenna squirmed around on Dylan's face as Jade continued to slam her wanton pussy down onto his rigid protrusion.

"My turn," Jenna said impatiently the moment Jade's climax had subsided. As soon as Jade slid off his cock, Jenna spun around and mounted him cowgirl. "I can't wait for this," she said and plunged Dylan's cock into her burning cunt.

"How's it feel?" Jade asked with a sly smile.

Jenna shook her head, eyes wide open. "Fucking awesome," she replied in a hoarse whisper.

She closed her eyes then and focused all her attention of that magnificent cock deep inside her steaming tunnel. His length filled her completely and really stretched her lips wide around its thickness. Every stroke was absolute heaven. She'd almost forgotten just how good a dick could feel. Juice flooded her cunt and trickled down Dylan's shaft as she once again rose up to the tip.

When she opened her eyes she saw that Jade had perched herself on their male lover's face, where she rocked back and forth on his rampant tongue and hungry lips. Jade leaned forward, cupped Jenna's shoulders in her hands and clamped her soft, wet lips onto Jenna's. Immediately their tongues got active, and the sensation of a tantalizing wet kiss while Dylan's cock filled her pussy was almost too much pleasure to take.

With her mouth salivating and her vagina drooling, Jenna vigorously bounced up and down on the cowboy's pleasure pole while feverishly tonguing Jade's mouth. Both women gasped and moaned as they kissed, their most erogenous zones getting stimulated to the max.

"I'm gonna come again," Jade announced after parting lips with Jenna.

"Lucky bitch," Jenna complained, still impatiently waiting to reach her first climax with the cowboy. She increased her tempo and reached behind herself so she could fondle Dylan's sack. As she fucked him with long, aggressive strokes she watched with envy as her girlfriend went through the throes of her second orgasm. When she was done, Jade reached between Jenna legs and started to rub the other girl's clitoris.

Jade said, "I'll give you a hand."

With both her cunt and her clit receiving full-on stimulation simultaneously, Jenna reached a crescendo within mere seconds. When she came her passage flooded with fresh juice that gushed out of her opening and all over Dylan's loins. He guffawed with both surprise and sexual excitement. Trembles rippled through her lust-gripped body and her head swam with desire. Jenna continued to slide up and down his very long shaft, massaging her tunnel while Jade's fingers rapidly strummed her clitoris. With a tremendous shudder, Jenna let out a howl that would have made a wolf proud. When her orgasm had finally subsided, she rolled off her lover and sprawled out on the blanket feeling totally exhausted.

"Are you okay, Babe?" Jade asked, lying down beside her.

Jenna nodded. "That was intense," she breathed. "Took a lot out of me." She grinned then. "It was worth waiting for, though."

Dylan was still lying where they'd left him, his erection raging and throbbing against his lower abdomen.

Jade nodded towards the cowboy's cock. "Help me make him come."

Jenna grinned again. "With pleasure. I love watching a cock spurt its juice."

The girls got down low either side of Dylan and took turns sucking the head of his cock really, really hard. He moaned and groaned and wriggled around on the blanket, barely able to withstand the intensity of their combined oral. Jade then used the slipperiness of their saliva as a lube to stroke the shaft in her hand while Jenna stimulated Dylan's balls with her fingertips. Within minutes his cock went really stiff and started to pulsate a moment before exploding the first thick wad of white cum. Jet after jet shot from his cock and splashed all over his body until his torso was literally drowning in it.

Jenna said, Wow!"

"That's a lot of spoof," said Jade.

Dylan lay back and just relaxed in the sun as the girls set to work drinking the warm cum from his skin and sharing it in a very wet and passionate kiss.

Milked by a Milf

"W e're going night clubbing," Tim announced when he and Ricardo showed up unannounced on Zack's doorstep that evening.

Zack lingered in the open doorway, leaning against the architrave. Both his friends were dressed for a night on the town, wearing predominantly black.

"I wasn't planning on going out tonight," Zack said, feeling a bit lethargic after working all day. "I was just gonna have a quiet one and chill out with a DVD."

Ricardo said, "Don't be so boring," and pushed past him and into the house. Tim tailed him inside and Zack turned to follow them into the living room, where the TV was on a sports channel.

"Well, where were you guys thinking of going?" Zack wanted to know, feeling just slightly curious.

"Somewhere different," Tim answered.

Ricardo said, "Have you got any beers?"

"Sure. In the fridge. Help yourself."

"Grab me one," Tim called out as Ricardo disappeared into the kitchen.

"And me," Zack chimed in.

"See," said Tim. "You're starting to loosen up already."

Zack shrugged. "I've just had a really long day at work, that's all. It's not that I want to be boring."

Ricardo returned from the kitchen armed with three beers. He handed one each to Tim and Zack. The three said cheers and started to drink up.

"You'll get in the mood to party once you have a few drinks in you," Ricardo said confidently.

Zack eyed his friends and asked, "You mentioned about going somewhere different. Where did you have in mind?" He sipped his beer and waited for an answer.

Ricardo provided it. "Tim and me found out about this club. Not one we normally go to, but apparently it's really good. Well, not that great for partying, but good for another reason."

Zack raised an eyebrow, but said nothing.

"It's full of older women looking to score with younger guys," Tim got to the point. "Namely us."

"Yeah, hot milfs and cougars," said Ricardo enthusiastically.

"How do you know they go there looking to pick up younger men?" Zack wanted to know.

"I know some dudes who have picked up there heaps of times," said Ricardo.

"And you've only just found out about it?"

Ricardo shrugged. "They wanted to keep it a secret. Greedy bastards. But one of them let it slip the other day." He glanced at Tim, then back at Zack. "And that's why we're here; to go out and snare us some experienced older women."

"I wonder what they look like?" said Zack.

"Word is most are pretty nice looking," Tim said.

"We'll find out when we get there," said Ricardo. "If it sucks we'll just go somewhere else." He thumped Zack on the arm. "Now, go and get dressed. We've got work to do."

Forty minutes later the taxi came to a stop about a block away from the night club they were heading too. When Ricardo paid for the fare, Tim said, "Zack and I'll get the first few rounds of drinks." The cab zipped off and the three men strolled along the crowded street, passing a couple of strip bars and, oddly, a charity shop nestled in between them.

Party-goers and revellers were everywhere and there seemed to be way more males than females about. Zack hoped that wasn't a sign of things to come. The trio stepped around a group of young women coming in the opposite direction and Ricardo let out an approving wolf whistle as the three men turned their heads to check out the girls from behind.

They crossed a side street and paused outside the club in question. Two burly security guards of Polynesian descent manned the door. The three scaled a dozen steps to get to the entrance and one by one they produced their IDs to prove they were of age. They were ushered inside where they each had to pay a ten dollar cover charge. After that, they were let loose in the den of cougars.

The music was current enough and there appeared to be quite a lot of women present. Zack was surprised how many keen smiles and looks he was getting as they made their way to the venue's only bar. There was a bit of a line up and it took a good ten minutes to buy the first round of beers.

"I say we knock this one down quickly," said Ricardo, speaking loudly above the thump of the music. "Then go and grab another. Get a buzz going quickly."

"We'll have some shots next time as well," Zack said, feeling quite keen to be out now that he was here and getting loads of attention. It was true the crowd was older, but there were quite a few lookers about. And the ladies certainly looked like they were dressed to impress with the goal of hooking up.

There was a raised section on the other side of the dance floor just near the DJ booth and the boys headed for that zone. There they found a spare patch of floor and stood there drinking beer and gazing down onto the dancers.

"She's pretty hot," Tim said and pointed to a rather stunning brunette dancing away, dressed in a tight black dress with a split along one side that ran all the way up to her hip.

As Zack looked at her she glanced his way, caught his eye and smiled. Both Tim and Ricardo slapped Zack on the back.

"She's hot for you, man," Ricardo said excitedly.

Zack shrugged nonchalantly. "It was just one glance."

"And a smile," Tim added.

Again Zack shrugged and polished off the rest of his beer. "I'm out," he said and slammed the empty bottle down onto a nearby table. "You guys wait here and mind our spot. I'm going back to the bar."

"Get some shots," Tim said.

Ricardo said, "And more beer."

It was roughly ten minutes later when Zack returned with a tray loaded up with six tequila shots and another three beers. He placed the tray down on the table and immediately all three men downed the first of the shots. Zack shook his head as the liquor burnt his throat. He took a sip of cold beer to douse the flames, then prepared to throw down the second shot.

It didn't take long for the tequila to get into his system and he was buzzing quite nicely. He just nursed the beer, taking his time with it and checking out the talent.

He felt a tap on his shoulder, and when he turned around he found himself staring into the smiling face of the brunette who had caught his eye earlier while dancing. He felt his heart skip a beat, not expecting her to come and seek him out. She was even more attractive up close and he figured her to be somewhere in her late thirties.

"Hi, I'm Jacqui," she said with another smile.

"I'm Zack."

He returned her smile and the two started chatting. A few minutes later the three guys were seated at a round table on the opposite side of the dance floor, where they joined Jacqui and her friends, Tina and Cate,

"I have two kids," Jacqui was telling Zack. "Two boys, aged ten and thirteen. Do you have any children? No, you're too young for that."

Zack shook his head. "Does that mean you have a husband?" he quizzed her.

She shook her head. "Not anymore. I'm divorced and happily single." She grinned and eyed him a little wickedly. "These days I more prefer, how shall I put it, *casual* encounters rather than anything serious."

"I can relate to that," he replied with a nod.

"My girlfriends and I often get together for girl's nights out. They're staying at my place tonight. My boys are spending the weekend with their dad, so we have the place to ourselves. Free to party!" she said with much exuberance.

"We should all go back to your place then and party on there," Zack suggested, noticing how well his friends were getting along with Jacqui's friends.

"That's the plan," said Jacqui.

Before Zack knew what was going on she was sitting on his lap with her arms wrapped around his neck and her lips and tongue hard at work ravenously devouring his mouth. He tongued her back with much enthusiasm and immediately felt his cock grow to full length inside his jeans. She was sitting right on it and it throbbed against her ass.

His hands caressed her back and he could feel her breasts squashed up against him. Jacqui kissed him like a starving woman. She was obviously extremely horny and in desperate need of a damned good fucking from a young man's cock!

"Let's go back to your place," one of the other women said to Jacqui.

Jacqui ceased kissing Zack and got to her feet, where she snatched up her handbag and took a hold of Zack's hand. The others paired up as well - Tim with Cate and Ricardo with Tina. The six of them couldn't all squeeze legally into the one taxi, so they had to split up and take several cabs back to the suburbs where Jacqui lived. Once there, the six filed inside and more drinks were poured in the kitchen.

As they drank wine, Jacqui said to the other couples, "You four will have to fight over who gets the spare room, but the kid's rooms are off limits." She waved her arm towards the expanse of leather lounge. "The couch is open for business." She whispered into Zack's ear. "You and I will fuck in my room."

Just the way she said that word made Zack's head spin with desire. His cock and balls were aching and he couldn't wait to fuck this woman senseless.

He drank from his glass and licked his lips. He then looked at Jacqui's succulent lips and couldn't resist, so he leaned forward and planted a kiss on her. Immediately she responded by thrusting her wet tongue down his throat and he happily returned the favor.

"Oh, get a room, you two," Tina complained and everyone laughed.

"I think that's a very good idea," Jacqui whispered to Zack and dragged him off down the hallway, where they entered the master bedroom at the end. She kicked the door shut, pushed Zack down onto the comfortable bed and pounced on him, once more ravishing him with wet kisses and loads of tongue.

His hands played with her beautiful ass as they kissed and he could feel the outline of G-string panties under her slinky dress. Jacqui ground her crotch against his raging hard-on and she kept gasping in his mouth as her excitement escalated with every passing second. He couldn't wait to feel her cunt so he slithered a hand between their grinding bodies and tried to get a feel.

Jacqui leaped to her feet and said, "Let me make it easier for you."

She quickly shed her clothing until she was completely nude. Zack couldn't take his eyes off her lush boobs and smooth cunt. His mouth watered in anticipation. She sure was one smoking hot older woman!

He whipped off his shirt and kicked off his shoes as Jacqui worked on undoing his pants and freeing his erection. She smiled when she saw his cock for the first time and readily tugged his pants down over his legs, where Zack kicked them away onto the floor. Jacqui's mouth got greedy and sucked his cock down her throat, swallowing every inch of it. She did this several times before letting him slip out of her mouth so she could use her tongue to lavish saliva all over his length and also his balls.

"Fuck that feels good!" he exclaimed.

"It's supposed to," she said easily and engulfed the head of his cock with her mouth again.

She didn't deep-throat him this time. Instead, she just concentrated on pleasuring the head with her lips and tongue while working his rigid shank up and down with her hand. Zack gently thrust into her mouth, watching with extreme interest as his cock slipped between her hungry lips. That was such a beautiful sight.

"Come sit on my face," he said. "I really need to taste your sweet pussy. Is it nice and wet?"

"Wet?" she was incredulous. "Of course it is! I'm positively soaked down there."

I'll find out just how wet in a second, he thought as she got into position above him and lowered her cunt onto his open mouth.

When he thrust his tongue inside her, Jacqui gasped and leaned forward to take his cock into her mouth again. She hadn't been exaggerating. Her pussy was soaked and he happily lapped up her juices and swallowed some. Before long her pussy was sliding all over his mouth as her juices made his face all slippery. She tasted just as delectable as any delicious dessert he'd ever eaten and, having her suck tenaciously on his cock at the same time, Zack was having the time of his life.

The feel of her big breasts squashed against his skin felt amazing and it motivated him to tongue her furiously. He had her groaning the entire time, and every time his cock slipped down the back of her throat, she made him groan as well.

Her cunt flooded with fresh juice and he couldn't believe how much there was. She was just as horny as he was and he just kept drinking from her well. He thrust his cock down her throat as she ground her pussy on his mouth. Now they were both moaning incessantly and it was getting very close to fucking time.

He pushed her off his face and gasped, "Ride me." Zack then deeply inhaled some much-needed air as Jacquie spun around and mounted him, guiding his cock into her opening and sitting down hard on it to drive it all the way inside her.

"That's better," she said and swooned. Jacqui closed her eyes and started to rise and fall like a gentle ocean swell. Zack took her tits into his hands and felt satisfied when the nipples stiffened into his palms. "You have a beautiful cock," she complimented him. "So hard. That's what I love about young cock. Never goes soft."

"You certainly know how to ride one," he returned, watching the lips of her cunt wrap tightly around his very thick shaft. Every time she rose up his length her pussy left behind a sheen of luscious juice, making his cock gleam.

"I've had plenty of practice," she admitted. "I love sex. Always have. Never understood these women who say they don't like sex or can't have an orgasm. I just think they've been with dud partners."

She fell silent then and just focused on the task at hand: Fucking Zack's cock.

Jacqui reached behind herself and commenced massaging his sack. At the same time she used the middle finger of her other hand to strum on her hardened clitoris. All the while she stroked fluently on his dick, never once losing her rhythm.

"I'm gonna come now," she said softly.

Jacqui was surprisingly quiet as she went through the pleasurable throes of climax. Although he really loved a girl who went nuts when she came, he quite liked the way Jacqui went about it. It was very sensual. She finished with a shiver and a whimper, then sat still on top of his cock and broke into a huge grin.

"That was amazing," she whispered. Dropping forward and squashing those lovely breasts against his body again, she kissed him on the lips and asked, "What's your favorite position?"

Zack thought about it. He didn't really have a favorite.

"I like them all," he replied.

"What about doggie? Do you love doggie? I do."

He nodded. "Sure I do. You want me to do you from behind?"

"I'd love that."

Again she planted a wet kiss on him, tantalized him with a flick of her tongue, then got onto all fours beside him on the bed. Zack eagerly got in behind her and took a moment to admire her immaculate ass and pouting pussy. So gorgeous. He probed the opening to her cunt with the end of his cock and teased her for just a moment. Jacqui grew impatient and pushed back onto his dick the next time he did this, effectively driving his length all the way into herself. They both grunted on entry and Zack quickly got into a fast and steady rhythm.

He slammed against her beautiful ass whilst clutching her hips in a firm grip. His balls swayed as he fucked her from the rear and her pussy made delicious sucking sounds as he plunged in and out with relentless vigor. He was actually surprised how tight she was in there, considering she'd had two kids. Jacqui was actually the first woman he'd had sex with who was a mother, so he had nothing to compare that too. However, he'd always imagined that bearing children would make things loose. Maybe he was wrong in that thinking.

"I'm gonna come already," Jacqui announced and let out a squeal as the orgasm struck hard and Zack increased his tempo and the ferocity of his thrusts. This time she was much more vocal as her body coiled up in tension and then released. Juice gushed into her passage and again her cunt made that sucking noise as he continued to fuck her really hard and very, very deep. He kept going until she couldn't take it any more and he ran out of steam. He then flopped back onto the bed and lay there breathing hard.

The sounds of sex echoed throughout the house and it was evident the other two couples were hard at it as well. Ricardo and Tina and Tim and Cate sounded as if they were having a fantastic time of it.

When Zack had his breath back and Jacqui had recovered

38

from her mind-blowing climax, she nestled in beside him with her back to him, parted her legs and guided the head of his dick back into her pussy. Lying on his side, Zack thrust into her gently with long, slow strokes, allowing them both to just relax and enjoy the sensation of his hard cock inside her soft, wet passage.

He didn't mind this position for some variety, although he didn't use it very often. It was quite relaxing, though, as well as being sensually fun. Jacqui had candles burning on the bedside tables and the dresser and the position suited the ambience created by the candles.

"That's going in nice and deep, Zack," she said in barely a whisper. In fact the sounds the others were making were overpowering any she and Zack mere emitting.

They continued spooning for a few more minutes. Jacqui never came, so Zack climbed on top of her and did her missionary, thumping into her vigorously now and rapidly building up her desire until she squealed in orgasm yet again. He couldn't help but smile as she came and came, admiring the look of pure ecstasy on her face and lust in her beautiful brown eyes.

"Don't come in me," she said when she was done. "That'll be a waste."

"How do you want me to come then?" he wondered.

"Lay on your back and I'll milk it from you with my mouth."

Zack grinned with excitement and got ready for it. It wasn't often a girl proposed to swallow his cum and he was really looking forward to it. The moment she started eagerly sucking his cock and stroking his shaft, he knew it would be a matter of mere minutes before he was exploding down her throat.

"You're getting me close already," he told her when he felt the tingles in his groin. "Here it comes."

He groaned as the jiz shot from his dick in powerful bursts. Jacqui happily swallowed every drop and finished with a smile as she licked her lips clean. She snuggled up in his arms then and Zack started to feel drowsy; both from the alcohol and the release of tension.

"Do you mind if I sleep here tonight?" he asked.

She kissed him on the cheek. "Of course not. I'd love you to."

Three's Company

"I envy you," Mia said to Angela in bed that morning. "I wish I didn't have to work today."

Angela stretched and yawned, feeling very relaxed. "I'll be thinking about you, Babe."

Mia kissed Angela on the lips and snuggled up close to her. "What are you planning on doing today, Babe?"

"I was thinking of going down the beach for a while," she replied, seeing a bright strip of sunlight at the edge of the blinds. "Relax, get some tan, maybe have a swim."

"Wish I could come."

"You have no problems coming," Angela said and chuckled.

"You know what I meant. But," Mia started nibbling Angela's neck, "speaking of which. Why don't you do me a favor and make me come before work?"

Angela kissed Mia's lips. "Only if you make me come at the same time."

"Sixty niner then?"

Angela nodded and the two girls tongued, causing Angela's pussy to throb. She could feel the juice flooding into her cunt with every luscious lick of her girlfriend's wet tongue. Mia's hand slid between Angela's thighs and she parted them so the other girl's fingers had access to her naked crotch. When three fingers entered her cunt, Angela broke the kiss and sighed with pleasure.

"Sit on my face and go down on me," Angela said, her eyelids now heavy with desire. She slid down the bed a bit away from the pillows and waited as her partner got into position above her and lowered her glorious shaven pussy down onto Angela's waiting mouth.

Yum, she thought as her tongue darted into her partner's very wet cunt. A moment later she felt Mia spreading her legs wider and her mouth clamping down onto her aroused dampness. When Mia's long tongue entered her, Angela gasped into Mia's mound as pleasurable tingles swept through her body.

Angela rocked her hips back and forth against her lover's mouth, loving the friction of Mia's chin against her clitoris. Both girl's tongues were running rampant as their desire increased. Angela was hungry and she greedily sucked juice from Mia's passage as Mia did the same. Already she could feel tension building in Mia as she worked her lips and tongue all over Mia's horny cunt.

It only took a few more minutes for Mia to come on Angela's face. She squealed into Angela's muff as the explosion of climax ripped through her. For a moment she stopped licking and just gasped over and over again.

"Don't stop now, Babe," Angela urged. "You almost had me there."

Immediately Mia went back to work to bring Angela to an

orgasm as well. When it arrived, Angela peeled her mouth away from Mia's pussy and smiled. Small squeals of pleasure escaped from her throat and she gently bucked her hips to thrust her cunt hard up against Mia's expert mouth.

"That was such a nice way to start the day," Angela said when her climax had passed.

"It was," Mia agreed and got out of bed. "But, unfortunately I can't bask in the afterglow with you. I'm gonna be late for work if I don't get a wriggle on." She wiggled her ass for emphasis, making Angela giggle.

A half an hour later and Mia was gone for the day, leaving Angela sitting out on the balcony of their highrise apartment sipping on a cup of tea all alone. The skies were clear apart from the odd cotton ball of fluffy white cloud.

She finished her tea and returned to the bedroom to get dressed, slipping into a white thong bikini that was so skimpy it barely covered her 'bits'. Downstairs in the basement parking lot she got into her car and drove out into the sunshine.

The journey to the beach only took about five minutes and, being a week day, finding a parking spot close to the sand didn't prove difficult. Walking barefoot down onto the beach, relishing the feeling of sand between her toes, Angela spread her towel out in a secluded area at the base of the dunes, stripped out of her shorts and top and flopped down onto the ground. She propped herself up on her elbows and gazed down at the water through the dark lenses of her sunglasses.

There were a few surfers further out catching a small swell, while inshore people were scattered about in the shallows; a mixture of guys, women and young children. About thirty meters away to her right Angela saw a couple of young men catching some rays. They looked lean and tanned.

It had been quite a long time since she'd experienced a man in the physical sense. She hadn't always been exclusively a lesbian. She had only adopted that status since meeting Mia and entering into a relationship with her. Prior to that she had very much considered herself to be bisexual. Mia had been the same, enjoying both men and women alike before entering into an exclusive all-female relationship with Angela.

"Two years," Angela said to herself as she rested her head on the towel. "Two years since I've had a real live cock."

She closed her eyes and just let the sun warm her skin. It was nice outside, not too hot. As she relaxed her mind started to drift and fantasies entered her thoughts. Scenarios from the time before meeting Mia played like a movie through her mind. Wondrous sexual encounters. As she recalled what it was like to be made love to by a man she felt herself getting aroused. Her pussy started to pulse and dampen, ultimately escalating to a point where it was throbbing with sexual energy.

She flipped over onto her stomach and tried to take her mind off sex by thinking about all things non-erotic. Still sexual images kept penetrating her mind. Angela glanced behind her at the ocean and thought she might need to take a swim to cool off in more ways than one.

Getting up off the towel she casually strolled down to the water's edge and let the ripples sweep over her feet. The water was cool, but not cold, so she stepped into deeper water until small waves were washing around her hips. A guy swam in on a wave and came to a stop beside her. He got up, smiled at her, then waded back out in search of more waves.

Angela dove under the next wave and exited out the other side coughing and spluttering as some salt water went down her throat. When she had that under control she attempted to catch as wave, but failed miserably. Body surfing had never been one of her talents, and her swimming in general wasn't particularly powerful.

She watched as two young, fit guys came down from the beach and waded out into the surf. Angela felt like she couldn't take her eyes off their bodies and found herself craving some male attention more and more lately.

But what could she do about it? She was in a relationship with Mia. She wasn't about to cheat on her. No way. She loved Mia. Mia had been good to her in every way.

Angela sighed and dove in front of a wave, attempting to ride it back into shore. It carried her some of the distance and she walked the rest of the way out and onto dry sand. After toweling herself dry she slipped on her sunglasses and stood there gazing about the beach. She perved on a lone man coming down onto the beach wearing no shirt and with a towel slung around his neck. He had the chiseled physique of someone who spent many hours lifting weights and eating a low-carb diet.

"Mm," she mumbled softly as she continued to watch him wander down to the water.

This was getting harder every day. Angela was really craving a real live cock. She missed that. Sure, she and Mia often played with their colourful array of dildos and vibrators, but it wasn't the same. They were just toys and there was no life in them. Besides, a real dick was also attached to a real body and she missed touching and being touched by a man.

Angela shook her head and tried to not only take her mind off sex in general, but especially off men. There was nothing she could do about that craving. She was committed to Mia and that's all there was to it.

Back home she took a shower, spent a bit of time tidying up the place, then spent the remainder of the afternoon reading an adult romance on her iPad. When Mia finally arrived home from work they went and got some Malaysian takeaway from the place down the road and brought it back to the apartment to eat. A bottle of red wine was opened and poured to go with the meal.

While they had been waiting for their meal in the takeaway, Angela had found herself checking out the Asian guy behind the counter. She wasn't really attracted to Asian men generally. She obviously just had an itch really bad at the moment.

As they ate their dinner and drank wine, Mia chatted idly about her day at work. It sounded like the day had involved quite a few frustrating hassles.

"You must be tired," Angela said and looked at Mia with concern.

Mia shrugged and sipped some wine. "I'll feel fine after a shower." She grinned a little wickedly then. "Don't worry, Babe. I'm not too tired to make love to you."

"Good," Angela said. She was looking forward to more sex, perhaps even break out the toys. She still had that yearning to be with a man, but she was keeping that to herself.

The pair watched a comedy on TV in the living room for a while, then Mia announced she was going to go take that shower. Angela followed her girlfriend into the bedroom, where Mia disappeared into the adjoining ensuite bathroom and closed the door.

Angela went to the bottom drawer of the dresser and removed a very long black dildo and a pink and white vibrator with clitoral stimulator. She then stripped naked and stood out on the balcony in darkness and gazed upon the city lights. A light breeze swept across the area and it felt lovely against her skin. She inhaled deeply of the night air, filling her nostrils with the scent of the nearby sea. When she heard the water stop running in the bathroom, she went back inside and lay down on the bed to await her lover. While she waited she picked up the black masturbator and ran a single finger up its long length from base to tip. She wished it was a real cock.

Perhaps, when Mia was pounding her pussy with this thing,

she would fantasize about it being real; that she was being fucked good and proper by some hunky guy. Like that muscly one from the beach.

Mia stepped nude from the bathroom and smiled when she saw Angela was ready for her and had several toys laid out for them to play with.

"I've been thinking about you a lot today," Mia said as she snuggled in close to Angela. "That orgasm this morning really helped me get through the day. I love starting the day off like that. We should do it regularly before work."

Angela nodded. "We will."

The pair wrapped themselves up in one another's arms then and kissed wetly, passionately and rather noisily. Angela felt the stirrings in her cunt and immediately juice flooded into her eager passage. She was grateful as hell when Mia started to finger her and she readily returned the favor, loving the way her partner's lower lips were all slippery with juice as well.

They broke the kiss and both girls gasped as their pussies were pleasured by exploring fingers. Mia's thumb rubbed hard over Angela's clit and she shuddered from the exquisite sensitivity. Mia picked up the vibrator and turned it on, where she proceeded to tease the entrance to Angela's passage.

"Feel nice?" she asked Angela and the other girl nodded. "You want me to plunge it inside you, don't you?" Angela again nodded. Mia thrust it inside just a few inches, then withdrew it again.

Angela closed her eyes and just enjoyed that warm buzz the toy was imparting on her horny pussy. With each penetration Mia plunged the plastic member in another inch until Angela's cunt was filled with vibrating bliss. She imagined a man was down there between her legs, plunging his thick, hard cock into her with eager thrusts. She felt the clit tickler stimulate her and it sent a series of shivering tingles all through her pelvic area. Mia banged it in and out of her hard now, thrusting the toy in deep, filling Angela's tunnel completely with its rigidity.

"That's gonna make me come in no time," Angela whispered.

As Mia brought her closer to a climax, Angela continued to fantasize that a real man was fucking her, and that a real cock was about to make her explode all over the bed.

Her body tensed up and started to shudder. She arched her back and thrust against the hand holding the vibrator. Mia jammed it in deep and Angela came with a scream of delight followed by another series of small, pleasurable shivers. She kept on bucking against the toy until she eventually lay still, where she stared up at the ceiling and sucked in deep breaths.

"Fuck that was good," she said and grinned.

Mia's mouth engulfed hers then and their hungry tongues lashed one another. Angela probed her lover's cunt with her fingers and immediately they were drowned in juice. She peeled her mouth away from Mia's and said in her ear. "I'm gonna fuck you with that big black dick."

49

"Ooh, please do." Mia rolled onto her back and opened up her legs. When Angela jammed the dildo mercilessly into Mia's cunt, Mia sucked in a sharp breath and groaned, "Oh my God!"

"Take it," Angela said aggressively and thrust the dildo in hard and deep, making her lover's pussy swallow eight inches of the massive ten inch length. "You want more? I'll give you more." Angela jammed it in until almost the entire fake cock had disappeared inside Mia.

The other woman restlessly squirmed around on top of the bed. Her eyes were shut and an expression of intense pleasure was etched on her face. Mia squealed as Angela plunged the tool in and out endlessly. The black rubber shimmered in the lamplight, all soaked in Mia's juice. Her cunt made squelching sounds as Angela continued to fuck it with a passionate tenacity.

"I'm gonna come," Mia announced and released a howl that would have made a pack of wolves proud.

The girls maneuvered into a sixty nine position after Mia had settled down and rather leisurely tasted one another's soaking pussies. Angela's tongue worked its way in and out of Mia's passage with methodical regularity. Mia sucked on Angela's clit and made her shudder with pleasure, but just a little bit of pain, too.

Mia was on top and her hips rocked back and forth, massaging her pussy on Angela's face. Angela ran her tongue all over Mia's clitoris before plunging it inside her lover's hot cunt once more.

"Thrust a finger in my cunt," Angela said between nibbles on Mia's puss.

"You do the same," Mia instructed her girlfriend and virtually both girls fingered each other's passage at the same time.

Angela felt herself quickly building to another orgasm with her pussy being stimulated by lips, tongue and fingers now. In no time at all she lay quivering beneath the other woman. Angela gasped and took Mia's entire cunt into her mouth, where she proceeded to suck it hard. Mia came on her face, her tunnel flooding with more juice and Angela happily drank it all.

"God, that was good," Mia said as she flopped onto her back on the mattress, her face all shiny with cum.

Angela couldn't resist. She moved in close to her lover and proceeded to lick her own cum off Mia's chin, cheeks and lips. Mia then returned fire and did the same to Angela.

"I love our sex," Angela said as they relaxed in each other's arms.

"So do I, Darlin'," Mia assured her.

Angela hesitated for a spell. She wanted to get something off her chest, but really hoped her partner didn't react negatively to what she had to say. Eventually she took a deep breath and just said it.

"Do you ever feel like there's something missing, though?"

Mia said, "In our sex life?"

"Yes."

51

"Like what? A cock?"

"Yes."

Mia pondered this for a moment. "Sometimes I do miss a real live cock, I must admit, but I'm very happy with you."

"I know you are, and I'm equally as happy with you. I wasn't referring to our relationship as a whole, just the sex part. I don't know, I've just been missing men in that way lately. It's been so long."

"So long since a man fucked you?"

"Yes."

"Same here," Mia conceded. "And if we're being open and honest here, then I sometimes miss being well fucked by a hunky guy as well."

Another pause, then Angela went on. "Do you think it would be wrong in any way if we occasionally included a male in our lovemaking?"

"Having a threesome, you mean? Nothing behind each other's backs?"

"Yes, a threesome, where it's all out in the open and consensual between us."

Mia said, "I guess that could be fun. Just so long as neither one of us gets jealous when the other is being fucked by a lovely big dick."

"So," Angela said slowly, "does that mean you'd be up for it?"

Mia nodded and kissed Angela on the lips. "Sure.

Occasionally. Let's just try it once and see how we feel about it. If we both enjoy it we can do it more regularly."

Angela smiled, feeling her pussy throb at the prospect of being filled with a big, hard cock again.

"Now we just need to find the right guy," she said.

"I think I might know someone," said Mia. "There's this guy at work, very good looking. I think he might be perfect."

* * *

Mia had arranged for her friend from work to come over on the Friday night. All that day at work Angela had not been able to keep her mind off sex, and she spent the entire day walking around with a soaking wet pussy. Her cunt was gagging to be fucked by a cock again and she couldn't wait.

Finally it was time to go home, where she ate a light meal with Mia and the pair took a shower together. When they'd done their hair and applied some makeup, they both dressed in sexy lingerie and stockings, covering themselves up for now with silky robes. Back in the kitchen Mia poured two glasses of chilled white wine and the girls went out onto the balcony to drink and take in the cool night breeze.

"He'll be here soon," Mia said and looked at Angela. "Are you excited?"

"I sure am. Can't wait, to be honest."

"Same here. I've been feeling toey for a man lately as well."

"So he's definitely attractive?" Angela said with some concern, fearing she just might not have any sexual connection with the guy. "He's not fat or anything?"

"No, definitely not fat. And," she kissed Angela on the cheek, "definitely good looking. Pleasant personality as well. Trust me, you'll like him." She grinned then. "Mark's pretty damned excited about the prospect of sleeping with two gorgeous women. He'll look after our needs, there's no doubt about that."

At that moment the intercom buzzed and Mia dashed inside to let Mark up the elevator. She waited by the entrance door for him to come up while Angela remained out on the balcony slowly sipping her wine. She heard the man arrive and Mia greeted him quite vivaciously. Angela took a deep breath and stepped into the living room.

Mark *was* rather handsome. He was tall with dark hair and penetrating blue eyes. The skin of his face was lightly tanned and his body looked very scrumptious in blue jeans and a fitting white T-shirt. He was quite well-muscled, like that dude on the beach the other morning.

"Hi," Angela said brightly as Mia introduced the pair. They kissed on the cheek and Mia dashed into the kitchen to get drinks.

"Need another wine top up, Babe?" she asked Angela.

"Sure." Angela produced her glass and Mia refilled it and her own.

"Would you like wine or beer, Mark?" Mia asked their guest.

"I'll go a beer, thank you, Mia."

When everyone had a drink they got settled in the living room. The girls sat side by side on the lounge while Mark took a seat in one of two adjacent armchairs. The stereo was on in the background, the volume set to low so they could comfortably converse.

The entire time they enjoyed their drinks and chatted, Mark kept eyeing up both women hungrily. At one time Mia casually pulled her robe up her thighs and parted her legs, allowing his roaming eyes to catch a glimpse of her cunt only partially hidden by lacy white panties. Angela did the same, keen for this man to have a good perve on her. She wanted him to desire her, needed him to be desperate to fuck her. He kept licking his lips as the flirting display went on and Angela didn't miss that bulge expanding under his jeans. He was getting very hard and he looked quite big.

"I'm getting a bit hot," Mark suddenly said and stood up to remove his shirt. At the same time, as the girls feasted their eyes on his tanned and muscular body, they slipped out of their robes, leaving themselves in bras, panties and stockings. "You ladies are smokin'!" he quipped and licked his lips yet again.

Mia unashamedly spread her legs and ran a finger up her slit. "You want some of this?" she said to Mark. She then leaned over Angela and pulled her panties aside, exposing the smooth lips of her cunt. Mia said, "And this?"

Mark looked like he was in some sort of trance as he eyed their aching vaginas. Again his tongue darted out of his mouth as he licked his lips for the umpteenth time.

"I need to taste that," he said, referring to Angela's cunt.

"Do it then," said Mia. "But get your clothes off first. I wanna suck on your big dick while you eat out my girlfriend."

Mark quickly dropped his pants and underwear, leaving his erect cock in full view. Now it was Mia's and Angela's turn to lick their lips. As their male lover homed in on Angela, she whipped off her panties, cupped her thighs in her hands and spread her legs as wide as she possibly could. Meanwhile, Mia slipped down onto the carpet and positioned herself so she could suck Mark's generous cock while he devoured Angela.

The moment Mark's mouth latched onto her mound, Angela gasped. Mark groaned at almost the same time as Mia gobbled up his cock and slid it deep down her throat.

The entire time Mark was tasting her pussy, Angela found herself feeling jealous that her girlfriend had his beautiful cock in her mouth. Not jealous that Mia was sampling a man, but jealous that it was in Mia's mouth and not her own.

Soon, she told herself. Just enjoy the oral Mark is giving you for now.

She reached behind her and unsnapped her bra, tossing it onto the floor. Mark's tongue plunged into her cunt and went to work on her passage like a soft, wet buzz saw. His pointed nose massaged her clitoris at the same time and Angela felt like she just might be able to come all over his face.

"God, I want some cock," she heard herself say somewhat

unconsciously.

At the sound of her words everything changed. Mia got up and stripped out of her underwear, leaving herself dressed in stockings only. Mark knelt between Angela's legs and nudged the head of his cock into her open cunt. Mia hovered over his shoulder to watch his entry into her gorgeous girlfriend. Mark thrust several times and completely buried his eight inch length.

Mia smiled at Angela as she looked up at her. "How's his dick feel?" Mia wanted to know.

Angela grinned. "Indescribable. Amazing. Awesome. I can't tell you how much I've needed a real cock and a real man."

"Enjoy it, Baby," Mia crooned and moved in close to her on the lounge, where she proceeded to sample Angela's nipples while Mark drove his fat, hard, hot and throbbing cock into her depths.

"I feel like screaming," Angela gasped. "It just feels so fucking good."

Every time he penetrated her fully Angela felt his balls slap against her ass cheeks. She loved that. Her plan was to have one orgasm on his cock now, then have a damned good suck on it.

"Fuck me," she said to Mark. "Ram that big prick into me." To Mia, she said, "My cunt is on fire, Babe."

"Good," Mia said and kissed her lips, her tongue darting down Angela's throat.

Angela wrested her face away from Mia's and said, "I'm gonna come already."

"Good. Do it. Come all over his cock."

Mark grinned when he had Angela in the grip of the most intense climax she'd had in months.

"Oh fuck! O fuck!" Angela screamed repeatedly as she thrust herself against her lover. His cock penetrated her deeply and the feel of it inside her was driving her wild with desire. Her climax seemed to go on and on and left her exhausted when it finally passed. "Fuck that was good. I so needed that." Angela sucked in a couple of deep breaths, then said to Mia, "Help me suck him."

With Mark seated between them on the lounge the women set to work pleasuring his magnificent love wand. Angela gratefully sucked it first as Mia's hand fed it into her mouth an inch at a time until she'd swallowed more than half of his length. It had been so long since she'd done this, but felt she hadn't lost her touch. She sucked him for thirty seconds of so, then relinquished the cock and it slipped into Mia's greedy mouth.

Angela took the opportunity to taste Mark's heavy balls. She sucked one testicle into her mouth, then tasted the other. Her tongue then rose up his length again and the two girls licked at the head before Angela took it down her throat for the second time.

Mark was moaning and groaning constantly. When Angela glanced up at his face she saw his eyes were closed and his features looked intense. He was loving every second of having two hot women licking and sucking on his knob and balls.

Mia wrestled the cock off her and devoured it while Angela stroked the shaft. She used her other hands to toy with his sack and jerked him off at the same time.

"Oh...Fuck!" Mark hissed. "Why don't you ride it, Mia? You must need it inside you by now."

"Yeah, Babe," Angela encouraged her. "Sit on his dick. I'm gonna sit on the floor here and watch you ride him."

Mia straddled Mark while Angela held his cock in an upright position and guided it into her girlfriend's tight cunt as Mia lowered herself onto it.

"That looks so fucking hot!" Angela said as she sat on the carpet to watch the show. "Man that looks hot!"

Mia was already panting as she slowly rose and fell on Mark's monumental tower. He cupped the cheeks of her firm ass and helped Mia to thrust down onto him. Angela couldn't stop smiling as she watched Mia's cunt continually swallow every inch of Mark's rigid flesh.

"Fuck it harder," she encouraged her girlfriend. "Come all over his cock, Babe."

"I don't think it'll take long," Mia gasped and increased her tempo.

Unable to resist, Angela moved in really close and wrenched Mark's cock out of Mia, where she proceeded to suck on it, much to Mark's pleasure. Angela relished extracting Mia's juice from his cock. She ran her tongue all over it, gave it one last suck, then inserted it into Mia's soft folds once more.

While Mia continued to fuck him, Angela climbed aboard his face so he could tongue her cunt again. The position was a little awkward as she tried to balance on the edge of the backrest, but she managed to keep herself stable so their male lover could pleasure her puss with his tongue while he pleasured Mia's pussy with his cock.

"Your tongue feels so nice in there," Angela swooned. "How's his cock feel, Babe?"

"Fan…fucking…tastic!" Mia gasped as she slammed herself down onto Mark's erection. "I'm gonna come…in a minute."

"Do it, Baby," Angela said.

Mark just mumbled his assent into Angela's muff.

Angela hopped off his face and gave Mark an enthusiastic tongue kiss. She then did the same to Mia before grabbing hold of her bouncing breasts and continually talked dirty in her lover's ear until Mia exploded with a scream of ecstasy. Her body convulsed and her thrusting slowed. She kept on shivering, bucking occasionally, then finished off with a long and very satisfied sigh. She smiled and climbed off Mark's member, dropped down into his lap and sucked her own juices from his cock. Angela joined in the feast until they'd licked up every delicious drop.

"I'm gonna ride him reverse cowgirl," Angela said excitedly and got into position. Mia fed his dick into her wanton cunt and Angela slid her pussy down the long shaft until only his balls were showing. "Fuck!" Angela said in a long gasp.

Mia kept massaging Mark's sack as Angela moved fluidly up and down, enjoying the sensation of being completely filled with hot male meat and being able to control the strokes. She went long and deep, sometimes pausing at the top of her stroke to allow Mia a chance to run her tongue up and down Mark's shaft. At one stage Mia removed his cock from Angela's pussy and gave it a really good suck before inserting it inside her girlfriend once more.

"How beautiful does that look," Mia mused, an excited smile splitting her face from ear to ear. She rubbed Angela's clit, then Mark's balls some more. "Gorgeous pussy, beautiful cock and lovely balls. They go so well together."

Angela closed her eyes and focused all her attention on what she was experiencing downstairs. The sensations his magnificent member was inflicting on her cunt were fantastic and she felt the tension starting to build within her. She kept her thrusting firm and steady, knowing that very soon she was going to feel herself approaching a climax and she couldn't wait. Stroke by exquisite stroke she built it up until her cunt was throbbing with arousal.

She let out a squeal as the orgasm unleashed and her body started to shiver. To help her out, Mark commenced pounding into her from below, thrusting his big cock in hard, heightening her euphoric state. When Angela was done she just sat there on his dick for a few moments while she got her breath back.

Mark took Mia doggie on the lounge after that, while Angela rested on the arm with her legs open so her partner could freely tongue her soaking pussy.

"Do you like fucking Mia?" Angela asked Mark as Mia continually moaned into Angela's cunt.

"Of course," he was adamant. "She's so tight and wet and so hot in there. Make's me feel like squirting my load."

"Soon you can," said Angela, "but don't come yet."

"I won't," he assured her.

Angela closed her eyes and moaned as she felt Mia's mouth sucking her lower lips before plunging her slippery tongue into her opening. Her pussy was quivering with excitement and she found herself wanting to be filled with that hard cock again. She placed a hand firmly on the back of Mia's head and bucked against her face.

Mia pulled away so she could let out a scream as she climaxed again. Mark was literally pounding the hell out of her from behind, making Mia lunge forward with every powerful penetration. His body slapped against hers as she continued to squirm around in ecstasy.

When she was done it was Angela's turn. The girls swapped positions and Angela immediately sank her tongue into the other woman's cunt while Mark teased the opening to hers with the head of his dick. He gripped her by the hips and drove his shaft all the way inside with one aggressive thrust of his hips. Angela gasped and bit into Mia's clitoris. Perhaps a little too hard, going by the flinch and squeal of pain from Mia. Angela kissed her lover better while Mark got into a steady rhythm behind her.

"My God, you know how to fuck!" Angela said emphatically. "You have the best cock."

"Fuck her hard, Mark," Mia urged. "I wanna hear her screaming."

"Yes, please," said Angela.

She found it hard to concentrate on eating Mia while this wonderfully big cock was pleasuring her wet tunnel. It was giving her immense tingles of pleasure. She'd so needed to be fucked good and proper like Mark was doing. She also loved the way his loose balls kept slapping against her with each deep stroke. He was going to make her climax again shortly. That was inevitable.

She intermittently tongued Mia while the other girl furiously strummed her own clit with the middle finger of her right hand. Mia orgasmed at exactly the same time as Angela climaxed on Mark's throbbing member.

Several positions and another orgasm each later, the women decided it was time for Mark to come. They got him to sit on the lounge while they first took turns sucking like crazy on his dick. Then Mia took over and worked his shaft in her hand, massaging it and coaxing the cum from his balls. Angela, meanwhile, aided his stimulus by lightly tickling his ball sack. Mark half smiled, half frowned as collectively the girls built him up to an intense eruption.

And erupt he did, his cock spewing forth heavy loads of milky white cum that splashed all over his chiseled chest and defined abs.

Angela giggled with excitement as she watched the spectacle, then helped Mia lick his skin clean, finishing off with a very wet and tasty tongue kiss.

Later that night once Mark had left, the girls made love in the bedroom, after which they cuddled up nice and close to enjoy the afterglow together.

"I've so enjoyed tonight," Mia said. "I felt perfectly fine with sharing you with a man. How about you?"

"Same. As much as I love you, I do need a hard cock every now and then."

"So do I," Mia admitted. "That's why I plan to make this threesome thing a regular event." She giggled then. "Men do have their uses."

Sixty Nine

The morning sun creeped in around the edges of the closed blinds. When it touched Tara's eyelids they fluttered open and she squinted against the bright light. An arm fell over her side and she twisted her head to see Dean had just awoken himself. He was a friend of hers and they had an understanding. While they were both single they would service each other's physical needs from time to time. Last night had been one of those times.

"I've gotta get up and go to work," he groaned.

Tara giggled and said, "Glad I don't have work today."

She watched as Dean got out of bed and started to get dressed. Her eyes scanned over his fit, naked form and she smiled. How he was single, she didn't know. He was a great guy and quite attractive. For some reason, although they were good friends and the sex was great, things just never transpired into a romance between the pair, and Tara doubted it ever would. Some things just weren't meant to be. It wasn't for them to analyze, but rather just go with the flow and what will be will be.

When he was fully clothed he bent over the bed, kissed her on the cheek and left, leaving Tara to daydream about the sex they'd had last night.

She still felt very horny, despite her seven orgasms. It was her peak time of the month; that time when her hormones were buzzing and her libido was on high alert. Dean would be too busy to visit over the next few days, so she decided she may have to search out a one night stand to tide her over.

She smiled as she looked up at the ceiling. That could be pretty exciting.

Tara stayed in bed for another half an hour before finally motivating herself to go into the adjoining bathroom and take a wake up shower; something she did every single morning. When she was out, she slipped into a bathrobe and went to the kitchen of the small two bedroom apartment, made herself a coffee and took it out onto the balcony. There was a shady spot in the corner where she had a little two seater table. She sat down, took a sip of her brew and gazed out over the multitude of highrise buildings that surrounded hers. Not too far away was the glorious expanse of blue ocean and sandy beach.

On the table was a pack of cigarettes and a lighter. She extracted a smoke, lit it and inhaled deeply, always enjoying that first cigarette of the day. One day she would have to consider giving up the habit, she knew, but not today.

As she drank her coffee and smoked, Tara pondered what she was going to do about her predicament. Every time she moved the silky robe would rub against her naked flesh - especially her nipples - making her feel aroused. Between her legs her pussy throbbed. She desperately needed more sex.

Should she go to the beach and look for a likely suitor? Or

perhaps she could venture out to a bar or a club tonight and search for a pick up? There was also the possibility of the resort's pool downstairs. That often had guys hanging around it or in it. Usually they were tourists, which was even better for a once-off. No confusion on anybody's part of there possibly being more to it other than just sex between consenting adults.

She finished her smoke and downed the rest of the coffee, then went into the kitchen to make a second cup. This one she took into the bedroom to sip on while she got ready for the day.

Tara decided to hit the beach and take a look around, get a bit of light tan and maybe go in for a swim. It was a warm day, so the thought of a dip was inviting. Might also help to douse those flames of desire that burned within her. She dressed in a red bikini, a color she always felt went well with her slightly olive complexion and medium-brown hair. When the bikini was on she checked out her figure in the full-length mirror, turning from front to back, side to side. Overall she was pretty happy with her body. Her thighs could probably do with some more toning and there was just a little bit of flab below her belly button that she would love to get rid of, but other than that, content. Her breasts were a nice shape and size. She possessed quite wide hips, but they had a really smooth curve to them, and men had always complimented her on their shape, so she gathered from that feedback that they must look okay.

In a beige cotton beach bag with a palm tree embroidered on the side, she stowed her beach towel, cigarettes, a bottle of water, hat, sunscreen and house keys. Then she was out the door and quite enjoyed the fifteen minute stroll through town to the beach.

There were a fair few tourists about this morning, which was hardly a surprise. The small city in which she lived mostly revolved around tourism. Down on the beach it was a similar scene. The sands weren't crowded, but there were quite a few people enjoying the small waves that rolled into shore.

Tara chose a section of sand just south of the flagged and patrolled area. She spread out her towel, slipped out of her white cotton dress, then lay down on her stomach and lit up a cigarette. She was facing the water and scanned the shallows for any hot looking guys. If she managed to pick up down here she was hoping for someone around her age in their mid-twenties. She didn't want someone too young. She enjoyed a man with experience who was confident, knew how to please and could find his way around a woman's body. There were a few fit looking males out there, and she was sure it wouldn't prove too difficult a task to entice someone back to her apartment for sex.

After her smoke was finished she flipped over and let the sun play on her stomach. With her sunglasses covering her eyes she loosely placed her hat over her face and just lay there for a while. Her mind drifted, flickering through images of all things sexual. She felt herself lubricating as her pussy began to throb. She certainly had the itch bad at the moment.

After another short stint with her back to the sun, Tara got up and waded down into the water between the flags. It was a touch chilly, but would be fine after a few minutes when she got used to it. She moved past a couple of young guys and they openly checked her out as she went by.

Too young, she thought and dove under a small wave. She broke the surface on the other side and flicked excess water from her hair. This chill in the sea was very invigorating. Tara dove under a second wave. When she surfaced she found herself face to face with a man who was about her height, but had quite a stocky, well-muscled body.

"Hi," she said without hesitation and smiled.

He nodded and said, "How you going?"

Tara didn't miss his furtive glance at her cleavage. "You a local?" she asked. Now he quickly scanned as much of her as he could see above the waterline.

"No. I'm just down here for the day."

"With friends?"

"No. On my own. I'm Jeff, by the way."

"I'm Tara. Nice to meet you. Water's really nice, isn't it?"

They hung out in the surf and chatted for the next fifteen minutes or so. When they exited the surf Jeff grabbed his gear and brought it over to where Tara was. There they lay side by side, chatted some more and caught some rays.

"Do you have a girlfriend?" Tara started to get to the point.

Jeff shook his head. "No, not at the moment."

"Are you sure?" Tara searched his blue eyes. "I won't cut

another woman's grass."

"Yes, I'm sure. And just what exactly are you implying, Tara?" he asked with an uncertain smile. "Are you trying to pick me up?"

She shrugged nonchalantly. "Is it working? I really need the male attention. Hope that doesn't sound desperate, but a girl has needs."

Jeff grinned openly now. "So does a guy."

"I'm well aware of that." Tara lit a smoke and offered them to Jeff, but he politely declined. "I'm just after a one-off. Nothing more than that. Do you think you might be up for it?"

"Sure," he readily agreed and rather hungrily ran his gaze all over her figure.

"Good," Tara quipped and got up. "I don't live far from here. Let's go rinse off under the beach showers and go back to my place."

They did exactly that and were pretty dry by the time they rode the elevator to the sixth floor of Tara's building. As she inserted the key into the lock of her front door, Jeff chuckled and pointed to the apartment number.

"That's a good number," he said. "Sixty nine."

She grinned at him. "Could prove quite prophetic," Tara said and opened the door.

"I hope so," said Jeff as he tailed her inside.

"Where do you want to do it? On the lounge or in bed?"

Jeff eyed her curiously. "You're very upfront, aren't you?"

"Like I told you, I'm really horny and have needs that have to be satisfied. I'm not gonna beat around the bush." She thought about that last statement and smiled. "That could have connotations."

"Let's do it on the lounge, then."

Tara took off her dress and Jeff started to shed his clothing as well. When they were both naked Tara openly looked Jeff up and down and was pleased to see he already had an erection. His cock was quite long and thick and she knew it was going to feel great inside her wanton cunt. She pushed him down onto the lounge into a seated position and laid across his lap. Her lips and tongue immediately went to work on his member, kissing it, licking it and sucking it. It still tasted a little salty from the sea, but she didn't mind that. Seasoned.

"Fuck!" Jeff exclaimed in pure pleasure as Tara swallowed his entire cock right down to his balls. "How do you do that?"

"Practice," she said simply when she withdrew. "I really love sucking cock."

"Do it again."

Tara did as requested and took great delight in feeling that long, fat cock throbbing all the way down the back of her throat. She then concentrated on pleasuring the head while using her right hand to pump his shaft in and out of her mouth. Jeff kept squirming around on the couch, unable to sit still. She was really giving his horny dick a damned good sucking and he was obviously finding the intensity of her oral hard to handle. He placed a hand on the back of her head and forced her face down his length until she'd swallowed him whole again.

"Lay flat on your back," she said. "I wanna do a sixty nine."

Jeff quickly got into position and licked his lips in anticipation of the feast to come as Tara lowered her soaking wet pussy onto his mouth. She just sat there for a moment and relished the sensation of his tongue darting in and out of her passage. When he sucked and licked her clitoris she shivered, leaned forward, raised his cock and took it back into her mouth. She sucked him really hard, made him flinch, then felt his tongue vigorously exploring the depths of her passage.

"Fuck that feels good," she squealed, then sank his cock way down the back of her hungry throat.

Her hand massaged his heavy sack as she gave Jeff head with much enthusiasm. The trick to giving a good blow job, she knew, was to love doing it. And boy, did she love giving head! Jeff's cock was a fantastic specimen and she couldn't wait to have it plunging in and out of her needy cunt.

Tara throbbed on his face, feeling fresh juice flood her passage. Jeff greedily lapped it all up, then sucked her entire shaven pussy into his mouth. She had to pause in her sucking again so she could release a long moan of pure bliss. Tara just sat on his face and enjoyed what he was doing to her down there. She still had his dick firmly in hand and it beckoned her to suck it once more.

"Take it down your throat," he mumbled against her lower

lips.

Tara deep-throated him all the way to his balls again, held him down there for ten seconds, then very slowly withdrew until only the head remained inside her mouth. Her tongue went to work on the taut, sensitive skin, running rings around the head and probing the eye. As Jeff's tongue plunged into her cunt she plunged his cock down her throat.

"I'm gonna come," she announced and quivered on her lover's face. More juice drenched her passage and Jeff feverishly licked it up. When she was done, she said, "Now I really need to fuck it."

With Jeff lying exactly where he was, Tara put one foot on the carpet and the other up on the lounge. She lowered herself onto his waiting cock and mounted him from the side. As it slipped into her inch by inch, she gasped and groaned and felt shivers of immense pleasure ripple through her. When it was completely buried within her depths she paused and enjoyed the feeling of being completely filled with a big, hard and throbbing cock. His member was very hot and so was her cunt. Combined they created a searing fire of passion, lust and desire.

Tara moved up and down effortlessly. Her interior was so well-lubricated that it accommodated his very big dick comfortably. Her pussy walls throbbed around its girth and massaged it firmly. Jeff was groaning beneath her, content to lie back and take what she was dishing out. Tara gradually increased the pace of her humping until she was slamming herself down onto his rigid member. Her pussy made sucking sounds as she fucked his cock and her lips were stretched very wide around its circumference.

"Fuck it!" Jeff seethed. "Fuck it nice and hard and deep. I want you to come all over it."

"Don't worry," she gasped, her eyes wide with pleasure. "I will."

A few minutes later and she creamed herself all over his lovely wand. To help out with her climax Jeff commenced thrusting into her from below, driving his cock to the extremities of her passage. Tara squealed and gasped, her body shivering with every beautiful sexual convulsion. When she was done she hopped off and sat down.

Her lover didn't give her any chance to recover. He spread her legs wide apart, got between them and inserted his dick back into her hot cunt, filling her tunnel completely once more. Tara gasped when the head penetrated the very end of her passage. Jeff thrust hard and very, very deep. His face was a picture of concentration, a serious expression, one focused on the task at hand.

"I love fucking you," he told her. "You've got a hot body and the most gorgeous little pussy."

She grinned. "I love your cock. It's so big and hard."

Now he grinned. "All the better to fuck you with."

And fuck her he did. Relentlessly his dick pummeled her slippery passage, sending her hormones racing and her head spinning with desire and euphoria. My God, he knew how to give it to a girl!

Both of them were groaning as the heated sex continued. Their bodies slapped together with loud smacking sounds and occasionally Jeff would seize one of her breasts and roughly squeeze it before twisting the nipple with his fingertips. Everything he was doing, every touch, every delicious stroke of his cock, was driving her wild. She would come for the third time before long and she couldn't wait for her vagina to erupt in ecstasy.

"You're getting me close," she said. "I'm right on the edge." Jeff fucked even more aggressively, spurred on by her words. "That's it," she hissed. "That's it. Yes! Yes!"

Tara looked towards the ceiling and let out an animal-like howl as the tension was released. She bucked against him with everything she had, driving his cock in deep and forcefully. Her body quivered with each delectable wave of climax. She finished with a tremendous shudder and Jeff stopped thrusting.

When they both had their breath back Jeff took her from behind. Tara loved the angle that doggie provided and somehow he went in even deeper still. The feel of him in there was indescribable. There was nothing on earth that felt as fantastic as a big cock buried deep inside her horny cunt. This was exactly what she needed today. All those orgasms last night with Dean, and still she was as aroused as hell right now. Her appetite at the moment was insatiable.

"I love the way your balls are slapping against me this way," she gasped. "Spank my ass." Jeff slapped each cheek of her butt several times quite hard. It stung, but felt great at the same time. "Do it again," she ordered and he did. "Now fuck me until I have another orgasm."

As he gave it to her like a well-programmed love machine, Tara reached between her legs so she could both feel his balls and his shaft sliding in and out of her very wet hole.

What a magnificent cock and ball set! she thought. I couldn't have picked a better lover this morning.

"Why are you slowing down?" she demanded when his thrusting was reduced to a crawl.

"I was close to coming," he admitted.

"Don't you dare come yet," Tara was firm. "I'm not done with you. I need to come at least twice more first."

Jeff resumed pounding her passage vigorously once he had his ejaculation urges under control and pretty soon he had her on that exciting precipice where she knew she was about to explode.

Tara's fourth orgasm was intense, but didn't last as long as the previous three. Still, it was equally as enjoyable and when it was over it left her feeling like she still had one more in her.

"Lay down again," she said. "I want you to come in my mouth, but first I want to come all over your face again."

Once in the sixty niner position for the second time, Jeff immediately set to work bringing Tara to a climax, obviously keen to experience his own release. She sucked his cock slowly while waiting for him to get her there and, only after she quivered with release on his face did she really start to work his dick towards a goal they both wanted him to reach.

Jeff grunted as he squirted hard down her throat. There was a lot of it, but Tara didn't mind one bit. She enjoyed swallowing a man's cum and she drank every last drop from his cock.

For now her desires had been satisfied.

But how long was that going to last? She wondered.

Lose Your Inhibitions

"If you want to live a free and easy sex life, then you'll just have to loosen up a little," Shandi said to Taylor over a cup of coffee. "Look at Mike and I. We're attractive, I think, but we're not super models. And we have no inhibitions about getting naked in front of each other or anyone else."

Taylor sipped his cappuccino and licked a mustache of froth off his upper lip. He'd known Shandi and her husband for quite some time now and knew they were into the swinging scene; apparently often swapping partners at the parties they attended.

"I'm shy even just approaching women, let alone being confident in the bedroom," he admitted, feeling forlorn.

"You have sex, though. Right?"

He nodded. "Sometimes. But even when I get a girl into bed I'm self-conscious about getting undressed, and also about saying what I like and that sort of thing."

"But why?" Shandi threw up her hands in disbelief. "You are quite a good looking guy, and you're not overweight or anything." She thought for a moment, then said quietly, "Is it small?"

"What? No, not at all. It's a normal enough size, I think."

"Then what's the problem?"

"I don't know. A lack of confidence."

Shandi leaned across the little table and tapped him on the skull. "It's all psychological. It's all in your head. You just need to step outside your comfort zone, get more sexual exposure and build up your confidence and self-esteem."

"But how?"

"I just told you how. By stepping out, experiencing more. Believe in yourself."

Taylor went home after the coffee feeling even more despondent than he had before he'd spoken to his friend. He knew she was right. There was no reason for him to be so self-conscious and always doubting himself in that area. Girls actually did have quite a good time with him when he made some moves.

That evening he was still pondering ways to step out when his cell phone rang. It was Shandi.

"I've just been speaking to Mike," she said, "and I think we've come up with a few ways that will really help you."

"Such as?" Taylor didn't sound so certain.

"Come on over and we'll all have a drink and talk about it."

Taylor rather reluctantly agreed and disconnected the call.

The drive to their suburban home only took him about five minutes, and soon he was coming to a stop in their driveway. A light was on in the entrance and he walked up to the door and knocked. Mike ended up answering it. He shook Taylor's hand and guided him through into the comfortable living room. The TV was on with the volume muted, and soft mood music emanated from a set of speakers either side of the television. Shandi came in from the kitchen carrying a tray of snacks; crackers with red salmon, tomato, cheese and avocado. She placed the tray on the coffee table, where three glasses of red wine awaited their consumption. Taylor took a seat and found himself sitting beside Shandi on the lounge while Mike sat virtually opposite them in a matching chair.

Taylor picked up a glass, sniffed the contents, then titled it to his lips and took a sip. Kind of woody and sweet, but quite nice. A cracker was then placed onto his tongue and he proceeded to munch away. He quickly followed it up with a second.

He knew Shandi from work. The two had hit it off in a friendship kind of way right from the outset. And in the process of that bond he'd become great friends with her husband Mike as well. The two had always been pretty open about their sex life, and Taylor wished he could be the same. He didn't have a steady partner and didn't want one. What he really craved was lots of sex with variety and no inhibitions.

"Want us to tell you the first of our ideas?" Shandi asked Taylor, who was already onto cracker number three.

He shrugged. "Sure," and picked up a fourth.

"Do you find my wife attractive?" Mike asked him totally out of the blue.

Taylor was a little dumbfounded, not sure if it was some sort of loaded question. He glanced to his left. Shandi was a very attractive woman. In her early thirties she only had the faintest of lines in the corners of her blue eyes. Her long hair was dark and lustrous and she had quite a tight little figure with a nice sized bum.

"Yeah, of course she is," he said eventually.

Mike smiled and sipped some wine. "What I'm asking is, do you fancy her? Would she be the kind of woman you would enjoy having sex with?"

Now Taylor felt really uncomfortable. He didn't know how to answer that for fear of upsetting somebody or embarrassing himself. He felt a hand on his thigh and turned to look at Shandi.

"Do you or don't you?" she prodded him.

Taylor glanced back to Mike and nodded. "Yeah, she's sexy. I've always thought that."

Mike seemed happy with his answer. "Good. I'll tell you the first part of our plan then. Tonight, while I sit here in this chair, I'm going to watch you fuck my wife on the lounge."

Taylor's jaw dropped. "I can't do that with you watching. Besides, she's a friend."

"That makes it even better, doesn't it?" Mike said.

"If you do this," Shandi said, "I guarantee it'll go a long way towards helping you get over your shyness." She smiled at him. "I promise I'll be gentle with you."

"She's a great lover, Taylor," said Mike. "You'd be crazy to pass this up."

"Can I think about it?" Taylor said.

"No," said Shandi and she cupped his face in her hands and

81

started to kiss him.

The wine was circulating through his system now and it helped to calm his nerves. At first he resisted her kisses, but then he really started to enjoy it. He was very conscious of Mike sitting opposite them and watching his wife kissing another man. But then again, these two did this sort of thing regularly, so Taylor shouldn't let that bother him. Shandi's wet tongue slithered delightfully between his lips and into his mouth. He returned fire and pretty soon was engaged in a ferocious tongue kiss that was making his dick throb with uncontrolled energy. Her hands were all over him and seemed to be everywhere at once. When she wandered lower and lightly brushed across his cock, he shuddered with pleasure.

Shandi stopped kissing him and stood up. Mike was smiling with some amusement as his wife started to strip naked and Taylor's eyes were glued to her spectacle. When she was completely nude, Taylor looked down at her shaven cunt and unconsciously licked his lips.

"She looks good, doesn't she?" Mike praised his wife and looked at Taylor for confirmation.

Taylor said, "She looks hot."

Shandi grinned and pranced around in front of him, making Taylor drool. "You'd like to fuck this body, wouldn't you, Taylor?" She put a finger under his chin and lifted his head up so he was looking at her face and not her crotch.

"Yes," he heard himself slowly say. He felt like he was in

some sort of dream. He was feeling good. A little nervous still, but good.

Shandi straddled him on the lounge, grabbed both his hands and placed them firmly on her butt cheeks. She then kissed him again while grinding her cunt up against his erection.

Taylor couldn't quite believe this was happening, but he was glad it was. His hands squeezed those delectable butt cheeks as his tongue wrestled with hers. She sure knew how to kiss.

Man, he really wanted to fuck her now.

After a few more minutes of passionate kissing, Shandi got off his lap, dropped to her knees and began undoing his pants. Mike looked on with extreme interest. Taylor felt self-conscious about having his cock revealed, especially to Mike, but what the hell? It was far too late to back out now.

He quickly removed his shirt while Shandi stripped him of his shoes and socks. These were placed beside the lounge, then her hand went inside his pants and fished out his member. She pulled it free of his underwear and stroked the head lovingly for a few seconds.

"Get him naked, Honey," Mike instructed his wife. To Taylor, he said, "You enjoying yourself?"

"Yes." His voice was barely a croak. His throat was constricted with desire.

"Wait 'til she starts sucking your cock, mate," Mike said with a smirk. "You're gonna love it."

His pants and underwear were tugged down his legs and now

all was exposed. Shandi tossed his clothing on top of his shoes, picked up his cock and studied it.

"Look at it," she said, and moved to the side so Mike could see. "It's a beautiful cock, long and thick."

Mike nodded with approval. "You'd better see what it tastes like, Honey."

Shandi grinned. "If you insist."

The moment her lips wrapped around his shaft Taylor felt tingles of excitement ripple through him. She worked his shank up and down with her hand while raking her teeth lightly over the head. Shandi then proceeded to suck him really hard, making it impossible for Taylor to sit still. His length dropped down her throat until only his balls were exposed.

"Fuck me!" he said.

Mike grinned. "I told you. Isn't she the best at giving head?"

Taylor nodded. He couldn't take his eyes off the sight of sexy Shandi gorging his cock the way she was. She sucked and slurped and licked, drank the pre cum that was now leaking from the tip. Her right hand had a hold of his sack and she was busily twirling his nuts around in her palm.

"I'm loving this cock," Shandi gasped between sucks. She stroked it with her fist. "I can't wait to fuck it."

"Why don't you then?" Mike said.

"I will in a minute."

As Shandi sucked his dick some more, Mike added, "I can't wait to see it."

He smiled at Taylor and Taylor rather sheepishly smiled back.

A few minutes later and Shandi was done with sucking cock. She climbed back onto Taylor's lap and mounted him. He groaned as he felt his cock sliding into her hot and very wet depths. Never in his wildest dreams did he ever think he'd be fucking Shandi. And especially not with Mike watching.

"That looks great!" Mike boomed when Shandi rose slowly up Taylor's length.

Already he could feel her juices on his balls and it felt really nice. Her cunt went up and down a little quicker now. Shandi had her eyes closed and was softly moaning. Her moans turned into desperate pants when she increased her tempo further and Taylor commenced playing with her beautiful soft boobs. They were heavy and bouncy and he just had to suck on those delicious chocolate-colored nipples.

Shandi came all over his cock while he was busy tasting her titties. She clutched him tightly and screamed into his ear as her body shook. Still she continued to ride him until all the sexual tension had fled her being.

She jumped off him and turned around, mounting him reverse so Mike had a fantastic view of her cunt eating Taylor's cock. Shandi massaged his balls and felt his slippery shaft as once more she started to ride him.

Mike was grinning and leaning forward in his chair for a closer examination.

"How hot does that look?" he said. "Fuck him, Honey. Make yourself explode again."

Encouraged by her husband's words, Shandi pounded Taylor into the lounge. For the moment he'd completely forgotten about his inhibitions and just enjoyed the moment. Pretty soon she was squealing out in climax for the second time in nearly as many minutes. Taylor had hold of her smooth hips and was helping her to slam down onto his rigid shaft.

When she was done she bent forward and downed the rest of the wine that was in her glass. After she had extricated herself from him, Taylor did the same, really feeling like he needed more to drink.

"You like doing doggie?" Shandi asked hopefully.

Taylor nodded. "Sure. Let's do it."

"See," said Mike rather happily. "He's already sounding a hell of a lot more confident." To Taylor he said with a wink, "Give her a really good fucking, mate. She needs it."

When Shandi was in position on all fours on the lounge, Taylor spent a brief moment admiring the silky wet lips of her gorgeous cunt. Impatient to get back in there, he guided the head of his cock into her soft folds and thrust hard with his hips. His member rammed into her up to his balls and he instantly got into a good rhythm. Shandi was already panting with desire and that served to fuel his lust and urge him on to bigger and better things.

Taylor really gave it to Mike's wife, slamming his body into hers relentlessly. His balls were swinging around madly and slapping into her clit every time he penetrated her fully.

"Do you like the way he fucks?" Mike asked her, on his feet now and watching more closely.

She sighed with extreme pleasure. "He's a...fantastic fuck!"

Taylor brought her to her third orgasm several minutes later. The climax was so intense it left her shivering and exhausted. More wine was poured and the three had a quick drink while Shandi recovered.

Eventually she admitted, "I'm done for the night, I think. But don't worry," she said quickly to Taylor. "I'll make you come with my hand."

Taylor sat back and relaxed as Shandi nestled in beside him and went to work milking the cum from his cock. Mike was back in his seat now and looking on, his eyes expectant. Taylor felt the faint stirrings of climax in his balls and the sensation built rapidly. He sucked in a deep breath and let it out in a grunt as his hot cum started to shoot from his cock and splash all over his torso. Shandi jerked him hard until all the juice had left his sack. She was smiling broadly and so was Mike.

Taylor just sat there, still a little shocked that this had happened, but he felt very relaxed and content with it all.

"You two said that this was the first step to help me with my problem," he said to Mike and Shandi. "What's the second?"

* * *

"Will this just be all couples?" Taylor asked Mike and

Shandi as they arrived at the secluded beachside campsite.

Shandi looked over her shoulder. "No. There should be a few single girls and guys here too."

Tents, campervans and cars were scattered all over the sandy ground. Palm trees lined the beach and surrounded the makeshift camping area. A quick head count told Taylor there were roughly twenty or so people in attendance. From what he could tell, anyway. As he got out of the vehicle the sound of pounding surf reached his ears and he could detect the scent of salt on the breeze that came in from the ocean. He helped the others unload the car and they set up two tents not too far apart. A cooler was powered up by the car's ignition.

Taylor had a wander around, people constantly smiling at him and saying hello. He felt very welcome in this relaxed atmosphere. There were a few cute ladies about, ranging in age from early twenties to very early forties, he figured.

Even though there was no electricity in the area, surprisingly there were several beach showers and fresh water taps. He'd been wondering if he'd get to have any sort of wash while he was here. The showers weren't private. They were completely open, just a shower head attached to a pole of wood, with concrete surrounding a drain at the bottom. He figured, given the nature of this camp, that no one cared about privacy anyway. One thing he wasn't excited about, though. There didn't appear to be any toilets anywhere.

He rejoined Mike and Shandi, who were still setting up a few things.

"We're going to build a giant bonfire just down there on the beach," Mike said and pointed. "And a few smaller fires around the campsite to light it up. So we all need to go into the forest across the road and gather as much wood and kindling as we can find."

Just about everyone present went in search of wood. Taylor pretty much kept to himself for the moment and collected loads of wood and sticks. Dead palm fronds were stripped with a knife to use as tinder. Some little fires were set up at intervals throughout the camping area, while a mountain of dead wood was piled high down on the beach. By the time the group figured there was enough material to burn through the night it was late afternoon, and the sun was dropping perilously low on the horizon, very soon to be consumed by the sea. There were a few thin strips of cloud out there and the setting orb lit them up in brilliant hues of red, orange, yellow and pink.

"Isn't it gorgeous," someone said beside Taylor.

He glanced to his left and saw a beautiful young blonde woman. She was smiling as she admired the sunset.

"It is," he agreed, thinking she was even more gorgeous than the scenery.

"Are you here by yourself?" she asked.

"No. I came with some friends."

"I meant, are you part of a couple?" He shook his head. The girl extended a hand. "I'm Mandy. I'm a single as well."

Taylor shook her hand and introduced himself.

"Have you been doing it long?" he asked. "You know. Swinging."

She nodded. "For a while. I really enjoy the variety." She grinned. "And I'm a bit of a show off. I like people watching. How about you?"

He shook his head. "Just starting out."

"Really?" Mandy sounded genuinely surprised. "Be with me first tonight when things get going. I love helping out newcomers."

"Okay." Now he smiled. "Sure."

"And try not to be shy about it. I don't plan on having sex in private." She touched his arm. "You'll be fine. They're a nice bunch when you get to know them. Like one big happy family."

"That sleeps together," Taylor quipped.

Mandy grinned again. "That's exactly right."

As the sun disappeared and twilight set in the fires were lit, and soon the beach was ablaze with warm light. Food was brought out and cooked and shared around. Taylor sat down on a towel on the beach with Mandy beside him. He had a plate loaded up with sausages, small pieces of steak, fried egg, fried potato and tomato. This was washed down with a beer from the cooler.

Across from them and to the left, Mike and Shandi sat side by side with some friends, eating their meal and sharing a few laughs.

Taylor felt very relaxed and didn't have any qualms about getting naked with others around, he reckoned. He was looking forward to getting it on with Mandy. She was very sexy, and also very pleasant company. He enjoyed her personality and openness. She seemed like quite a nice girl.

As he ate he casually glanced about, checking out some of the other women and wondering if he would get any action from any of them. Possibly. No, probably, he told himself.

After dinner there was a mad flurry of activity as many stripped naked and dashed into the surf for a night swim.

"You wanna go in?" Mandy asked Taylor, eyeing him hopefully.

"Sure," he said and the girl immediately got naked. He couldn't help but have a good perve on her. She was smoking hot.

"Get your gear off, pervert," she said in good humor and ripped his shirt off over his head. Taylor took his own pants off and she held his hand as they strode naked into the water. "This is nice," she said when they were in waist deep.

The temperature of the sea was absolutely perfect and Taylor dove under a wave, loving the freedom of swimming naked. Mandy was completely wet now as well, and she jumped on him, wrapping her arms around his neck. A wave came through and very nearly knocked Taylor off his feet. He kept his balance and next thing he knew Mandy's lips were all over his.

As their lips parted and tongues tenderly touched, Taylor felt his cock stiffen and grow at a rapid pace. He ground it against her smooth cunt, causing her to break the kiss and gasp.

"Take me up onto the beach and fuck me," she said urgently.

Hand in hand they waded out of the sea and back to their towels by the fire. Most people were still out in the water, including Mike and Shandi, but some remained and were starting to get frisky. When Taylor sat down, Mandy pushed him flat on his back and immediately sat on his face, where she leaned forward and took his raging cock into her hungry mouth. Taylor furiously licked at her delicious passage. She was so fucking wet he just had to suck some of her cum into his mouth and swallow it. Meanwhile his cock slid down her throat and he could feel the fingertips of both her hands all over his balls.

Taylor sucked on her erect clitoris, making her shudder. She sucked his cock even harder while Taylor worked his tongue all over her hot and steamy cunt. He couldn't get enough of it and she seemed to be feeling the same way about his cock.

"That's the way, mate," he heard Mike's voice say.

Taylor smiled into Mandy's pussy and continued to eat her delicious minge.

Mandy was suddenly on her feet then, where she waddled down his body, picked up his cock and inserted the head between her pussy lips. Then she sank down his shaft and groaned with both pleasure and relief. Taylor grabbed chunks of her ass as she moved along his length. Glancing to the right he spied naked Shandi and Mike starting to play with another couple. He saw Shandi get on her knees so she could take another man's cock into her mouth. That man's partner returned the favor by going down on Mike.

His attention was then back on Mandy and the way her amazing and very tight little pussy was making him feel. She was massaging his cock quite beautifully and she really knew how to move. He reached around her body and cupped her lovely breasts in the palms of his hands. The nipples were nice and stiff, the surrounding flesh so soft and squishable. Mandy was panting and moaning, her sex sounds becoming more incessant as she increased her tempo and the tension built in her lithe little body.

Taylor thrust from below, driving his cock deep into her cunt. He sensed she was getting close to reaching a climax and he really wanted her to come on him.

"Oh...God!" she gasped as her body started to tremble. "I'm...coming."

Taylor slammed into her as she continued to bop up and down on him. Her climax was over as quickly as it had come on and she fell backwards into his arms. Taylor's cock sprang out of her pussy as he wrapped his arms around her warm body.

"I really like fucking you," Mandy said. "*Really* like it."

After a moment's rest Taylor did her from behind, enjoying the sight of his cock sliding in and out of her immaculate pussy and grabbing her great little ass at the same time. He could feel his cock going in nice and deep this way and Mandy really seemed to be getting off on it.

"Fuck me," she whispered hoarsely. He thrust into her a little faster. "I love you fucking me."

Taylor idly glanced about the beach and admired the scene as everyone now seemed to be involved in some sort of sexual situation. The fire glowed on naked figures everywhere, and the sound of sex filled the night air.

Mandy now had a hand between her legs and was groping at Taylor's balls. He liked that. It felt good to have them played with while his cock stroked her wet passage. Her hand then went to her clitoris, where she vigorously strummed herself, making herself moan and groan even more than she already was. Taylor upped his pace until he was thrusting into her with much aggression. He loved fucking this girl, was really having a great time here on the beach.

After she'd managed to reach another small climax, Mandy flipped over and Taylor made love to her while facing her. He liked this position as she could run her hands all over his chest and they could also kiss. Her hands caressed his pectoral muscles, where she lightly raked her nails over his skin. Taylor leaned forward and kissed her, his tongue hungry and keenly exploring her tasty mouth. As they pashed Mandy raked her nails down his back now, sending pleasurable tingles all through him. Taylor propped himself up on his elbows, deciding it was time for him to have his first come of the night.

As he worked away on her, the warmth of the night and the

heat emanating from the fire combined to make him break out in a sweat. He wiped it from his face with a hand, not wanting it to drip onto his lover. Just when he was about to explode he pulled out of her and emptied his balls all over her body.

Together they went over to the showers. One was being used by somebody else, so Taylor let Mandy use the vacant one first. She rinsed his juice off her skin and the salt from her hair. When Taylor stepped under the cool jet of water, Mandy kissed him on the cheek.

"Have fun tonight," she said. "Let's get together again later. Okay?"

"Sure."

She left then in search of some more action while Taylor was content to relax under the stream of water for a while. It was cool and refreshing and he was glad to finally get the salt water off his flesh. He smiled as he washed his face. His shyness and inhibitions seemed like they were in the distant past now. And Mandy! How fucking awesome was it to get to have sex with a hot babe? And so sweet at the same time.

He felt a hand on his now-flaccid cock and he saw one of the older woman standing beside him.

"Mind if I share your shower?" she asked.

"You can have it," he said. "I'm finished."

She shook her head and smiled lewdly. "No. Don't go away. I want a piece of you. I like meeting the new people." She moved in close, her lips only inches away from his. "If you

95

know what I mean."

They kissed openly and the woman's hands immediately went down to his cock, one stroking his testacies while the other wanked his dick back to a full erection.

"I'm Sharon, by the way," she said and kissed him again.

This time Taylor broke the kiss. "And I'm Taylor."

Sharon grinned. "Now that the formalities are over, I think you should take me down to the beach and fuck me senseless."

He didn't appear to have a choice. Sharon took him by the hand and literally dragged him back down to the fire. Taylor wasn't too sure how much energy he had in reserve right at the moment. It hadn't been very long since he'd come, but he was willing to give it a shot.

As they arrived at a blanket Sharon had on the ground, Taylor saw Mandy off to the side busily servicing two men at once with her mouth. She was down on her knees, a man either side of her, and she appeared to be really loving double the male attention.

Taylor found himself quite liking Mandy, yet he didn't feel the least bit jealous that she was having fun with others.

He lay flat on the blanket and Sharon went down on him. She'd only been sucking his dick for about thirty seconds when a younger female came over. The girl watched for a moment, then dropped to her knees.

"Do you mind if I share that with you, Sharon?"

"Not at all, Kat." Sharon held Taylor's dick out to the

newcomer and Kat wrapped her sexy lips around it.

Oh, God! Taylor thought. I can't believe I've got two girls at once here.

He was in heaven as the women kept swapping his cock from mouth to mouth. For a while he just kept his eyes closed, lapping up the brilliant and unique sensation. He'd never been in this spot before and he was so grateful to his friends, Mike and Shandi, for showing him this fantastic new way of life.

The younger woman hopped on his cock then while Sharon squatted down over his face and rested her soaking wet pussy firmly on his mouth. If Taylor thought things were incredible a few moments ago, then this scenario right now was totally insane!

Sharon's pussy was drooling on his face and he was only too happy to drink from her luscious well. All the while he could feel Kat's exquisitely-tight little muff sliding all over his throbbing dick. She was panting and Sharon was moaning, their sounds mixing with the entire symphony going on around the fire. Taylor tongued Sharon deeply, then ran his tongue all over her happy clitoris. Kat was now rocking back and forth of his member, grinding it into the very end of her tunnel and giving her clit some stimulation. She came a moment later, after which the girls swapped places.

Kat's pussy was so tight, even on his tongue. Sharon mounted him reverse cowgirl and immediately adopted a fast rhythm. Kat squirmed around on Taylor's mouth, constantly pleasuring her clit and slit. She had a hand behind her and was clutching a hunk of his hair. Sharon was going to town on his cock, slamming herself onto it relentlessly, not slowing down for a second. She was going for gold, Taylor was sure, and at this rate it wouldn't take her long to reach her goal.

Both women arrived at a climax simultaneously and the air was filled with their combined screams of immense pleasure. Kat got off his face when she was done but Sharon refused to stop.

She turned her head and said, "I want you to come in my cunt."

"Okay," Taylor was readily agreeable.

By now Kat had vanished and he was left alone with Sharon. She hopped off his cock and turned around, wanting to face him now while she humped him into the sand. With a broad smile she sank down his shaft yet again and kept staring deep into his eyes as she rode him. She was quite an attractive older woman and Taylor found himself getting rather lost in those deep brown eyes of hers. The firelight danced on her irises and it looked sexy as.

"Make me come," he said to her. "I wanna feel it squirt deep inside you." He couldn't believe how open he was being. This was exactly how he wanted to be.

"I want to feel that just as much as you do," Sharon assured him, still maintaining the eye contact and never wavering.

She increased her pace, lifting her ass up and down and

fucking him like an expert. She was obviously very experienced and had probably had sex multiple thousands of times throughout her adult life.

Taylor had some serious catching up to do.

It all starts tonight, he silently vowed.

A few minutes later and Taylor was shooting his load deep inside Sharon. She still held his gaze and he saw the satisfaction in her eyes, knowing she'd reached her goal and made him climax.

"Fuck I love a man's cum in me," she said and licked her lips.

When she hopped off him Taylor ended up with his own mess all over himself and he dashed off for yet another shower. On this occasion no one seduced him while under the water. Returning to the scene of the action he spied Mike encountering a similar situation to what he'd just been involved in. Both Shandi and another woman were hunched over him as he lay prone on the ground. They shared his dick with much enthusiasm, as if it were the best tasting thing on earth.

Taylor went into the main camp area and grabbed a beer from the cooler. A small fire burned just meters away, painting his naked skin in subtle shades of red and yellow. It was quiet where he was and he needed a little bit of chill out time to recharge. Already he'd done three women. He was keen to do a few more. He was sure he could manage at least one more climax before he was done for the night.

Over the course of the next hour and a half Taylor had sex with four more women he hadn't yet fucked, deciding to share himself around. He held back from ejaculating as he did the rounds, saving that for the very last hurrah.

At the end of the night he found himself back with Mandy. They were both pretty taxed by the time they came together again, so they decided to spoon; a much more relaxing position than some others. Mandy didn't reach a climax while Taylor fucked her, but he was determined to have his last orgasm of the evening with her. She was his favorite.

He stroked into her methodically, ever so slowly building himself up to a crescendo, and didn't bother pulling out this time. He just kept going, unleashing his warm seed deep within her pussy.

The pair went down to the sea for another swim after that, where they splashed about having fun in the waves.

"You know," Mandy said as she wrapped her arms around his neck. "I think we would make a pretty good team. It's nice to have a steady partner while enjoying this lifestyle. Most others have. What do you think?"

Taylor found himself nodding in the darkness, the idea suddenly really appealing to him.

He said, "I think I'd like that."

Aroused

L ucy held husband David's hand as they walked through the parking lot. He was tall and she was tiny. He had black hair and she had blonde.

"Do you think this will help?" she said.

"I hope so," David said. "I don't know what's going on with us these past few months, but for some reason we seem to have both lost our libidos."

"Us both being busy with work and the kids has drained us, I think," Lucy said, almost to herself. "I really don't think it's anything physical."

"Psychological." David nodded. "Probably. We've just been too mentally drained to really get turned on." He kissed her on the forehead as they walked. "Which is why I thought this party might help stimulate our minds."

"I don't want to get involved," Lucy was adamant. "I just want to observe. Swinging is not really my thing. I don't like to share in that way."

"Neither do I, as you know. I've already talked about that to the organizer. She said it's fine just to come along and watch. It's totally up to us what we do and don't do."

"I am feeling kind of excited about this," Lucy admitted. "More curious than anything. Hopefully it stirs up our hormones.

Then we can go home and fuck like rabbits."

"It'll get our focus back on sex, I'm sure," David was confident. "That's all it is. We just need to have sex on our minds more and that'll increase our sex drive."

They were about to find out if the swinger's party would help. The venue was a converted warehouse in an industrial area and they'd just arrived at the front door. Inside, behind a counter, the organizer was there to greet them. Another couple were just going through.

David introduced himself and Lucy to Cartier.

"I'm afraid I still have to charge you the admission fee," the beautiful older woman said. "Even though you say you just want to watch and not play."

"That's fine," David said agreeably and whipped out his wallet. "We understand." He paid the fee, returned his wallet to his back pocket, took Lucy by the hand again and they went on inside.

Music was playing at a comfortable volume when they entered the main area. Rooms had been built on either side, furnished with beds and all necessities required for playtime. Up the far end was a dance floor, to the right the bar area and the common area was furnished with tables and chairs, as well as some comfortable lounges.

A quick glance around told David all the bedrooms were currently empty, everyone present in the common area having a relaxing drink and a chat. So far the guests were fully clothed and no action of a sexual nature was taking place.

"I feel nervous," Lucy said, clutching David's hand more tightly.

"Why? We're just going to be having a look. Let's go get a drink."

At the bar David purchased a beer for himself and a wine for his wife. They took a seat on one of the comfortable lounges and watched as more patrons entered the club. The music had gone up a decibel or two, but still easy to talk over.

The ratio of men to women appeared to be quite even and David wondered if only couples came here. Did any single guys or girls come along? Or were only couples allowed?

Nearly half an hour had passed and they were onto their second drink.

"I'm getting a little bored," Lucy said, breaking the silence that had stretched between them. "Nothing's happening."

David sighed. She was right. It was all pretty sedate so far. If something didn't eventuate soon, then they would be out of there, having achieved nothing.

"It'll heat up," he said, turning towards her. "Maybe we picked a night where everyone's a little on the shy side."

"I hope not," Lucy was blunt. "I came here to see people fuck." She downed the remainder of her wine. "Get me another drink."

David looked at her sharply. "Yes Sir."

She put a hand on his arm. "I'm sorry. I didn't mean it to

come out like that. I'm just feeling a little frustrated here." Lucy leaned over and kissed him on the lips, after which David got up, went to the bar and returned with fresh drinks.

He nodded towards the dance floor, where two couples were dancing and seemed to be getting pretty friendly. They watched as the women came together and started touching each other up while their men looked on. A minute later and the four went into one of the bedrooms. They didn't close the door, which meant they didn't mind if people wanted to watch. David saw clothing slowly being removed until all four climbed onto the bed completely nude.

"I think it's warming up now," he said to Lucy with a grin.

"Shall we move down for a closer look?" Lucy said.

Before David could respond Lucy was on her feet, drink in hand, and making her way down to the room. David got up and followed her, standing behind her in the doorway. No one else in the place seemed interested in taking a look, but a glance around and David saw a few others starting to kiss and touch each other up.

The two men in the room were sitting at the head of the bed with their backs against the wall. The women were presently going down on them and it appeared they had switched partners. Both guys watched their partners suck the other man's dick. David felt his own dick start to grow as a result of the visual. He'd seen his fair share of porn in his life, but this was the first time he'd ever witnessed other people having sex in the real world.

The girls were enthusiastic about their work, heads bobbing up and down with great pleasure. Both guys were groaning as their cocks slid in and out of hungry mouths. Lucy put her hand on her husband's back and David felt it move down onto his butt, where she playfully squeezed one of his cheeks. She was starting to get just a little aroused and excited, he realized, and the knowledge increased his own arousal until his cock was a throbbing entity inside his pants. He slipped an arm around Lucy's shoulders and drew her close to him.

"I'm liking this," she whispered in his ear and flicked her wet tongue over his lobe. That simple action sent a shiver of excitement through him. Her hand squeezed his ass again.

The action on the bed changed. While one women continued to suck cock, the other grew impatient and mounted her man. David watched, mesmerized, as he witnessed that lengthy dick being swallowed up by an obviously very wet and willing pussy. The guy still receiving oral watched his woman ride another man's cock and a satisfied smile crossed his features.

David couldn't imagine being happy about seeing Lucy screw another guy. That wasn't the purpose of their visit to this place. He didn't imagine she'd be too keen on seeing his cock inside another woman's cunt, either.

"I'm hard," he told his wife.

Lucy's hand ventured around to the front of his pants, where she proceeded to massage his erection through the material.

"Very hard," she reported. "Mm."

"Is it turning you on watching this?"

She looked into his eyes and smiled. "Yes. I'm getting nice and wet down there. My pussy's throbbing."

Her very words made his dick throb and she felt that. Lucy gave it a very firm squeeze, then let it go and continued to watch the show.

Both couples were fucking now, the second guy mounting his lover from behind and doing her doggie with vigorous thrusts of his hips. Both women were moaning loudly, loving every second of the pounding they were getting.

David heard the sounds of sex coming from somewhere behind then and he glanced over his shoulder. He spied two men doing one girl on a lounge, while another guy was sitting in a chair and had two women sharing his cock in an oral frenzy.

Things started getting more wild on the bed. While one man lay prone, one of the women mounted him while the second man got in behind and entered her ass. The second woman squatted down on the prone man's face so he could lick her pussy. The room was filled with grunts and groans, moaning and panting as the four fucked in what looked to David like a very awkward scenario.

Lucy's attention had been diverted to the sex taking place in the common area. David saw her watching, with much interest, the two women giving ferocious oral to the man in the chair.

Lucy clutched his arm and whispered hoarsely in his ear,

"My cunt is throbbing. I really need you to fuck me."

"Let's get a room," he suggested and took her by the hand.

They chose one about halfway up, entered and immediately started to undress.

"Should we close the door?" Lucy said when she was down to her bra and panties.

David shrugged. "Depends if we want privacy."

Lucy smiled a little wickedly then. "I'm feeling adventurous. I don't want anyone to join us, but I kind of don't mind if someone wants to watch." She undid her bra and dropped her knickers. "It's exciting."

David shrugged again. "Okay. We'll leave it open then. I'm game if you are." He dropped his pants and underwear and climbed naked onto the bed.

"Look how big your cock is," Lucy said with another grin. "You *are* excited."

"It needs to be sucked by my very hot and extremely sexy wife," he told her.

"Really?" On all fours Lucy slowly crawled up his body until her face was only inches away from his. "How do you know I want to suck it?"

"Because you love it," he said with confidence.

"Are you sure about that?"

Now he grinned. "I'm sure."

They kissed then, lightly at first without tongues. Then their mouths opened simultaneously and they engulfed each other.

Now tongues were running rampant, eagerly licking inside mouths and tasting each other fully. David grabbed the sides of her head and really tongued her furiously, overcome with lust and sexual hunger for his beautiful wife. Lucy's hand traced a line down his torso until her fingertips were touching the head of his horny cock.

David broke the kiss and gasped. "That feels nice. Grab hold of it."

Lucy did as he asked, clutching it in a firm grasp. "So hard," she said with some admiration in her voice. "I think it does need to be kissed and sucked."

"It does," he assured her. "It needs to slide down your throat."

"I'd better give him what he needs then."

She went down low and David watched as her wet tongue ran circles around the head, sending tingles of excitement and anticipation through him. Her fingertips tickled his balls and he could feel them swirling in their sack.

Outside the room the sounds of people having sex were intensifying. To David it seemed like there were more people out there now. Some new ones must have arrived.

Lucy's keen mouth plunged down the length of his shaft until his cock had completely disappeared down her throat. She withdrew slowly, then thrust his cock down her throat again. Still her fingers toyed with his sensitive sack.

"Suck it," he groaned and Lucy spent some time fixated on

the head of his cock, using her lips and tongue to inflict immense pleasure on it. "That's it," he encouraged. "I love that."

Her mouth was noisy as she worked away on his member, and the sounds she was making were really turning him on. It had been a while since they'd done anything sexual, and the last occasion it had seemed like they were just going through the motions out of duty rather than latent desire.

A young and very attractive woman appeared in the doorway and observed proceedings for a moment.

"Would I be able to join in?" she asked hopefully.

Lucy paused and turned to her with a smile. "Sorry, but we're just going to play with each other tonight."

The woman nodded. "Do you mind if I just watch then?"

Lucy looked at David and he nodded.

Lucy said to the woman. "No. That's fine. You can watch."

David's excitement had instantly doubled now that they had an audience. Lucy returned to sucking his cock and the young woman seemed to take great pleasure in watching David being consumed by his wife. The girl put a hand up her skirt and started rubbing her cunt through her underwear. When David saw this his cock throbbed inside Lucy's mouth.

"I think you should ride it," he said.

Lucy said nothing. She sucked his cock for another twenty seconds or so, then climbed onto it and penetrated her wet interior until he was in up to his balls. As she slowly moved up and down his shaft, Lucy started to moan.

"That looks so hot," the woman in the doorway exclaimed. "Watching you two is making me so wet."

Lucy grinned down at David and began humping his faster and harder until her body was slapping against his flesh and the bed was bouncing around like a trampoline.

"I'm gonna come," she announced after only several minutes of vigorous humping. "Oh...God!"

Her climax was intense, but short-lived. When she was done, she fell forward and the two tongued ravenously again. By the time they stopped kissing the girl in the doorway had vanished.

David chuckled. "I think she got so horny watching us that she had to go and find some action of her own."

He rolled and flipped her off him then. Feeling like going down on his wife before fucking her some more, David buried his face between her parted thighs and greedily lapped up the juices from her soaking pussy, reveling in how sweet she tasted. Before long he had his wife moaning again and she kept moving around restlessly on the bed as his tongue lashed her cunt and clitoris.

She bucked against his face as David's tongue plunged into her relentlessly. He could barely breathe, but he didn't care. She tasted so good and it was making his cock throb uncontrollably. He felt like he hadn't had sex in years, he was that aroused.

"I need to fuck you some more," he said and slipped into her in the missionary position. His cock went in and out like a piston, thrusting into her depths and throbbing deep inside her lush tunnel.

"Fuck me," his wife urged. "Fuck me hard, baby. I wanna come all over your cock again."

Liking the sound of that, David really gave her the pounding of a lifetime, fucking her the way he used to when they first got together. Lucy was loving it and he had her screaming in climax in no time flat.

A couple was now standing in the open doorway to watch the hot action, but Lucy and David were barely aware of their presence. They were too embroiled in their own passion and pent up desire.

She sucked his dick again, ramming it down her throat like her life depended on it. After her quick-fire oral, David took her doggie and watched his cock disappear inside her cunt once more. She was the wettest she'd been in such a long time and coming to this party had proven to be a fantastic idea. David took a hip in each hand and bucked into her with deep, aggressive thrusts. He then adopted a smooth rhythm, gradually increasing the speed of his strokes and occasionally varying the depth.

The couple in the doorway were cheering them on and David used this as motivation to give it to Lucy even harder. His body slammed into hers, driving his cock to the very extremities of her tunnel. Her tits swayed beneath her as their fucking caused her body to rock back and forth. She clutched the sheets tightly in her hands as once more her sexual tension mounted and built towards yet another shattering climax.

It came in shuddering waves. Lucy moaned and squealed, groaned and moaned some moved as her body was rocked to the core. David's opinion was that it was the most intense orgasm she'd ever had with him and it was greeted with cheering and clapping from the doorway. He glanced over his shoulder and saw that there were now five people crammed in the passageway.

To give them a show, David and Lucy spooned next, facing the doorway so everyone had an uninterrupted view of his thick cock stroking her wet cunt.

"That looks beautiful," one of the women commented. "I need to go find a cock to fuck." She disappeared, leaving just the two couples.

David whispered in Lucy's ear, "I really need to come."

"Do it," she encouraged.

"When I'm about to come I'm going to pull out and shoot it all over your body so they can watch."

She grinned at that. "Okay."

David concentrated on the feelings he had down below. His cock was so desperately horny and he really needed a release. He stroked Lucy's pussy slowly and methodically, feeling his ejaculation starting to build. When the tingles intensified he fucked her hard for a few strokes and pulled out of her at the very last second, shooting his hot load all over her stomach in powerful squirts. Once more their audience cheered and applauded. David squeezed the last drops of cum from his cock and dribbled them onto Lucy's cunt. He finished with a satisfied sigh, lay back on the bed and grinned up at the ceiling. The crowd dispersed now that the action was over and went in search of their own fun.

Lucy lay on her side and propped herself up on her elbow. She kissed him on the cheek and said, "I think our plan worked. That was the best sex we've had in years."

"I'm not in any hurry to go home," he said.

Her eyes lit up. "Then let's do it again."

Porn Star

She was in a factory, perched on a rather uncomfortable bench top with one guy doing her pussy while another dick was thrusting into her mouth. However, the discomfort of her surroundings was completely offset by the pleasure she was experiencing right now.

Kandy Kane had an extremely high sex drive. She was in the perfect job to not only satiate those desires, but earn great money in the process.

The stud at her cunt was told by the director to open up her legs a little more and thrust slower while one of the cameras got a close up. Kandy took the opportunity to give her mouth a rest for a few seconds. Her lips were feeling stretched and getting a little sore. That tended to happen after so long repeatedly sucking a dick.

Her smooth pussy was on fire. She didn't wax it completely, but left a small V of black hair down there. She thought that looked sexier, more womanly than being completely bald. The actor's cock was quite big and very thick. Her cunt was soaked and she was sure the sounds it was making as it was being fucked were being picked up by the boom mike. She flicked her long blonde hair over her left shoulder as another camera moved in close to her face, preparing to capture some intimate shots of the oral action. Bright lights shone on angles from either side of the set. At the moment they felt comfortably warm, but sometimes, in the peak of summer, they were too damned hot.

"Fuck me!" Kandy screamed, both for the sake of the movie, and because she was feeling so fucking horny right now.

The stud beside her nudged his dick back into her mouth and she repeatedly deep-throated it, much to the actor's pleasure.

If anyone thought that all porn was acted and no one was enjoying themselves, then they had a serious misconception. Kandy loved fucking on camera just as much as off. Maybe even more so. And so did the guys. Everyone involved had a great fucking time of it.

A few minutes later the director said, "Let's go for some DP."

No, don't stop now! Kandy thought. I'm on the verge of a climax.

She gave a signal to the director to indicate this and he let the action continue on a little longer. There was nothing better than capturing a genuine female orgasm on camera.

She screamed when she came, having now removed the cock from her mouth for fear of accidentally biting it. Her pussy flooded as it was continually pounded. Kandy put a hand on her chest and tilted her head towards the ceiling, where she let out another wail of absolute euphoria.

She got to rest for just a moment after her climax, then it was time for double penetration. She wasn't complaining. It was one of the advantages of doing a MFM threesome.

The man she had been sucking sat on the edge of the bench and Kandy straddled him. She lowered herself onto his freshly-lubed cock and allowed it to slowly penetrate her ass until it was all the way in. Feeling only half full, she spread her legs wide and leaned back with her hands on the bench either side of her anal lover. The actor who had brought her to a wondrous orgasm stood between their legs and prepared to enter her pussy once more. He nudged the head into her entry and thrust deep inside.

Kandy couldn't help but gasp and a camera was there to capture her initial facial expression as she was penetrated. The guy behind her played with her big tits, adding to the overall pleasure. The man that fucked her cunt thrust hard, causing her to rock back and forth on the dick in her ass.

God! There was nothing better, she thought. Right now she truly was in sexual heaven.

Kandy came again in no time with two big hard dicks in her. What woman wouldn't in that situation? Her explosion was intense and a series of cameras were all trained on the three to capture every titillating bit of the action.

"Cut!" the director called after five more minutes. "It's time to go for the pop shots."

Counting breaks, the entire scene had been going for more than an hour. Now that she'd had a couple of orgasms, Kandy was just about ready to call it a day. A long, hot bath was awaiting her at home.

Kneeling on the cold concrete floor Kandy took a cock in each hand and took turns sucking each one while jerking off the other. The stud who had been inside her cunt just now was the first to shoot his load into her mouth. Kandy let it dribble out over her lower lip and down her chin. She quite enjoyed a man coming in her mouth, but preferred not to swallow it. Liked the sensation rather than the taste. The second guy took a little longer to reach a climax. When he did, Kandy aimed his cock at her tits and they copped a milky spray of warm jiz. To complete the scene she gave each man another quick suck, then smiled up at her lovers with a look of immense satisfaction.

An assistant gave Kandy some hot, moist towels to clean herself up with, then she started getting dressed, feeling just a tad stiff from all the different positions. She'd taken a real pounding at times during that scene, but she'd loved every delicious moment of it. There truly was no other career for her except this one. She was an adult star and that was all she wanted to be.

* * *

It was dark by the time she arrived home and parked her black BMW in the triple lock up garage.. She entered from the garage into the spacious kitchen, poured herself a straight scotch and took it out back where a pack of cigarettes were waiting on the table. The sun had just dropped behind the mountain range to the west. She lived in the hills and out back, when it was daylight, she had a magnificent view of the verdant valley

117

below. Some steps led down to a pool and deck area. She had the lights on and the pool water was rendered a tropical turquoise color.

Kandy took a seat, extracted a cigarette from the pack and lit it, taking great joy in sucking the smoke into her lungs. She chased it down with a sip of scotch that burned her throat. That also felt good.

Today's scene had been a good one. She'd really, really enjoyed her work today. Doing two men was probably her most favored scenario and she hoped to do another one soon. Right now her desires were satiated and she was glad she had five days off before her next booking. There was also a party on the weekend before then that she was really looking forward to. It was a get together for some of those in the industry. She knew from experience how events would transpire. It would end up one big orgy and she felt her pussy quiver at the very thought of that. Apparently several people would be roaming around with camcorders to capture the action candidly. It wasn't an official porn shoot. Just a fun party that would also been filmed.

She grinned in the night. There was sure to be plenty of studs there on Saturday evening. Again her pussy throbbed at the thought.

Kandy smoked a second cigarette while she finished her drink, then went back into the kitchen for a refill. This she took into the ensuite bathroom off the master bedroom and started filling the large spa bath. She stripped naked and sat on the edge of the bath while waiting for it to fill. When there was enough water in the tub she turned off the taps and slipped into the very warm water.

Immediately she felt tension and fatigue leave her body and she started to really relax. Picking up her drink she sipped from the glass slowly and felt like another smoke. There was no way known she was going to smoke in her home, though.

Her cell phone rang then. It was sitting on the vanity. Kandy reluctantly got up, dried her hands on a towel, picked up the phone and sat back in the bath to answer it. It was her manager. After the pleasantries were over with, he got down to business.

"What have you got on tomorrow?" he asked her.

"A few things planned," she said cagily. "Why is that, Derek?"

"I have a producer who's in a bit of a bind," Derek explained. "He's filming an outdoor scene tomorrow morning and one of the girls has called in sick. He specifically asked if you could fill in. He's even willing to add a little extra cash for the short notice."

Kandy took a deep breath. She was really looking forward to having a break tomorrow.

"I don't know," she said finally. "What's the scene?"

"It's in a field in the woods. Not that far from your place, maybe a twenty minute drive. It's a threesome scene. No major script to learn, just all action, really. Male, female, female. I know you don't mind doing girls."

No, she didn't mind at all. In fact, doing a girl and a guy might be quite nice. Not too many cocks to please at once. She hadn't done one of those threesomes for a few weeks.

"Okay. I don't see why not," she said into the phone. "What time?"

"Get there at ten for wardrobe and make up," Derek chirped. "And thanks, Kandy. You'll really be helping them out. Probably lead to some new work with fresh actors."

"Sounds good," Kandy said and disconnected the call.

She downed the rest of her drink and reclined in the tub until only her face was above the waterline. She wasn't bothered that she had a job in the morning, really. After all, it wasn't as if she wouldn't have a good time.

* * *

It was a beautiful day in the woods. The sun was shining, but it wasn't hot. Just a faint hint of a breeze was barely enough the rustle the long tufts of grass about the place. A rug was laid out in the clearing, around which all the equipment had been set up.

Kandy's hair and make up had been done and wardrobe had fitted her out with her attire for the scene. She felt a little silly in her park ranger outfit with tiny little shorts instead of trousers, but it was all part of the act. She had on a shirt with the sleeves rolled up, a matching hat, and big black hiking boots.

Basically the plot was this: The male actor, Carl, and other female actor, Samantha, would be getting it on following a picnic. That was where Kandy came onto the scene. She would

120

happen upon the couple while doing her dutiful rounds in the forest. Instead of insisting they behave themselves and get dressed, Kandy would happily join in the fun.

The filming got under way and Kandy smoked a cigarette while waiting for her cue. She watched as the couple - and they were both extremely attractive - indulged in a bit of picnicking. Carl was shirtless and well-muscled without being too big. Samantha was wearing teeny shorts that didn't even cover the cheeks of her ass. She had straight black hair that fell halfway down her back and an olive complexion.

Kandy lit another smoke as the sex action got underway. Layer by layer the clothing was shed until they were both starkers. They kissed and caressed, kissed some more. Carl spent five minutes devouring Samantha's pussy, much to the girl's delight, then she returned the favor and happily bobbed her mouth up and down on his lengthy cock. Soon she was squatting down on Carl and mounting him.

It was now time for Kandy to enter the picture. She swaggered on set, emerging from the woods as the cameras filmed her approach. Kandy deliberately accentuated her hip movement, overplaying the sexy.

"What's going on here?" she demanded of the lovers on the blanket.

Samantha gasped in surprise and quickly covered her breasts. "Honey," she said to Carl, "it's a park ranger."

Carl looked up at Kandy and tried his best to look sheepish.

Most porn acting - when not actually fucking - was pretty woeful, and Kandy was first to admit that. She tried hard not to laugh at their attempts to look surprised and embarrassed.

Samantha said to Kandy, "We were having a picnic. Then things got all romantic. We didn't think anyone was around."

"Well, you thought wrong," Kandy said, putting on a tone of authority.

"We'll put our clothes back on," Carl said quickly.

Kandy held up both hands. "Don't do that just yet." She focused her attention on Samantha. "Now, miss. What are you hiding down there between your legs? Hop off so I can take a look."

Samantha did as the ranger asked and got off Carl, revealing his big and very hard dick. Kandy squatted down beside him and took hold of his cock.

"Hm. Interesting," she said. She got down low and commenced sucking on it. When Samantha started to protest, Kandy turned on her. "Would you rather a fine, miss?"

Samantha shut her mouth and Kandy resumed her oral, working Carl's beautiful cock between her lips. She stroked his shaft up and down. It was still damp with Samantha juice and was really nice and slippery.

As she worked away on his dick she could feel her pussy filling with juice. She was throbbing down there and feeling very keen to get into the action now. She licked all over his shaft, sucked on his balls, then got to her feet.

To Samantha, she said, "Suck his cock again while I get undressed."

Samantha did as instructed while Kandy quickly stripped naked. She then pushed Kandy out of the way, straddled Carl in reverse, lifted up his dick and guided it into her willing cunt. He slid all the way inside in one go, filling her completely and making her pussy throb even harder.

"Your man has a very nice cock," she said to Samantha. "Why don't you be a good little girlfriend and got sit on his face. I'm sure he won't mind."

All the crew were watching proceedings and the cameras were capturing it all from various angles. Kandy was in her element and actually felt like she had taken control of both the scene and the set. The director seemed content to just go with the flow for the most part and Kandy liked that. It gave her more freedom to enjoy herself.

And enjoy herself she did!

She rode Carl's cock very hard, thrashing herself down upon it time and time again, increasing her pace with almost every stroke. Her cunt was flooded by now, leaving Carl's dick all shiny. Behind her Samantha was moaning as she squirmed around on Carl's tongue. Kandy herself was building to a climax now and she couldn't wait for it to arrive. She knew it would just be the first of at least two or three before this scene was over.

She put on an exaggerated show for the nearest camera when her orgasm arrived. Not that she really had to act. Her immense pleasure was all very real. With juice flooding her cunt, Kandy bounced up and down on Carl's cock while tilting her head back and screaming skyward. Behind her Samantha grabbed hold of her hair and yanked it, adding a tinge of pain to the pleasure.

When she was done she got off Carl and spent a moment greedily licking her own juices from his cock. She then rammed it down her throat repeatedly.

The director called for some doggie action. As Samantha got down on all fours and Carl positioned himself behind her, Kandy spread her legs in front of the other woman so Samantha could go down on her at the same time. She grunted when Carl entered her fully and started to stroke. Kandy watched the pleasure spread across Samantha's features as her lover got into a good rhythm deep inside her cunt.

Kandy then grabbed the girl behind her head and forced her face downward, where Samantha readily started to lick Kandy's needy and very horny pussy. The girl was quite good and had obviously done this a number of times before. She moaned as Carl really gave it to her and it sent tingles all through Kandy's groin area. She couldn't help but smile.

Samantha pulled her face away and screamed, "Fuck...me!"

Carl was busy spanking her ass now as he drove his long shaft into her with relentless vigor. Kandy watched the look of intensity on his handsome features. He really looked like he knew how to give it to a girl and she couldn't wait to be fucked *by* him, rather than just ride him.

124

Her turn came about five minutes later, just after Samantha had experienced a small orgasm. Kandy lay prone on the blanket while her lover knelt between her legs. Samantha lowered her steamy pussy onto Kandy's tongue and she probed the other girl's sweet passage as Carl thrust his magnificent cock into her hot cunt.

God, his cock felt good, she thought as Samantha rocked back and forth on her face. He felt so big and he was really starting to fuck her good and deep now. His rhythm was sensational and she knew it wouldn't be long before she came again. She tongued Samantha furiously and soon had the girl squealing in ecstasy. Juice trickled over Kandy's tongue and she swallowed it. Carl was continuing to pummel her tunnel with his adept technique and Kandy felt the stirrings of climax quickly build until she exploded all over his lovely cock. Just when her initial climax started to ebb another one came onto her, stronger than the previous. She writhed around on the blanket and could barely take a breath, the intensity of it was that strong.

The girls shared Carl's cock soon after, licking it, stroking it and sucking it down their hungry throats. Kandy continually toyed with the man's balls and he really enjoyed that. As they both ran their tongues over the head, Kandy and Samantha came together in a very wet and open-mouthed kiss that would look great on the video.

Once they'd each had the pleasure of being fucked by Carl once more, it was then time for him to come.

125

He stood on the blanket while the girls knelt before him. Samantha did all the work, stroking his dick until he was ready to ejaculate. Kandy just sat there waiting for it to happen.

"Here it comes," he told them and then started to grunt and groan.

Samantha aimed the eye of Carl's dick in the direction of Kandy's open mouth. She had her tongue out and caught the first few squirts of his load. Samantha then took the rest and the girls shared Carl's offering in another kiss. Samantha sucked the cum off Kandy's tongue and proceeded to swallow it all.

Kandy grabbed a hold of Carl's spent cock and took it into her mouth. He flinched when she sucked hard on the head, feeling hyper-sensitive after his ejaculation. Kandy opened her mouth wide and pushed forward, forcing at least six inches of his eight or so inch length down her throat. Ever so slowly she withdrew until she spat him out.

"That was awesome guys, girls," the director gushed.

He was surely gay, Kandy thought. Judging by his mannerisms and the way he spoke. He came over and gave Kandy a quick squeeze to thank her for her great last minute work. She relaxed in the warmth of the sun for a spell before getting dressed in her own clothing.

* * *

Saturday arrived and Kandy was excited. She was really looking forward to tonight's party. It would be a lot of fun. These parties always were. She was feeling very randy now and hadn't had sex since that scene in the woods two days ago. Two days sometimes seemed like a long time to her. Still, it had been good to have a couple of day's break.

In the morning she had some chores and shopping to take care of. During the afternoon she did some personal grooming; waxing, plucking and various other necessities. By late afternoon she was getting ready to go.

It was a pool party, so underneath a light summery yellow and blue dress she had on a white bikini with a G-string bottom. It was one of her favorite pieces and she knew she looked really hot in it. After slipping her feet into some casual flat shoes, she snatched up a towel and her handbag, then went to the garage and climbed into her car.

The party was at a producer's mansion atop a ridge on the opposite side of the valley to where she lived, so it was a fairly long drive to get there. Kandy had her car stereo blasting all the way, playing dance tracks that always put her in a positive and energetic frame of mind. When she finally arrived there were already quite a number of cars parked in the massive driveway and out on the street. After finding a spot, she got out and strode purposefully up to the front door. It was open and she stepped inside.

Most of the guests were already out back, but she spent a few minutes saying hello to those that were inside. The restaurant-sized kitchen was a hive of activity as chefs and kitchenhands prepared trays of food to be circulated among the guests. In the bar area just off the living room waiters and waitresses were dashing about popping bottles of champagne and loading up trays with a colorful variety of alcoholic beverages and mixers.

Kandy ventured outside where she followed a path that cut through a lush lawn area and onto the massive pool deck. There were tables and chairs everywhere and loads of deck chairs; some on the lawn and some on a large expanse of wooden decking. A plethora of lighting about the place gave the whole scene a glow without being too bright. People were everywhere. Adult stars, directors and producers. The pool itself was set lower than the deck and at one end was a big spa already filled with people. As with her own home the pool overlooked the valley far below.

A glass of expensive bubbly was handed to her and she turned to face Jack. He was one of the male actors, and she'd had the pleasure of working with him on at least four or five occasions.

"Looking forward to a big night?" he asked her.

Kandy sipped her champers and nodded. "I need a big night. My body certainly does."

He grinned. "I'm sure you'll see plenty of action."

She shared his smile. "And I'm equally as sure you will, too."

Kandy lit a smoke and relaxed in a deck chair for a bit. Music began to play and some of the female stars started dancing on the grass. Kandy watched them idly for a few minutes while she smoked and drank, then she decided it was time to take a dip in the pool.

It was busy in there, but still plenty of space due to the size of the thing. There was a cascade down the far end and she swam down to it, allowing it to crash down over her head. A female actress she'd worked with before named Carly joined her under the torrent.

"Been working much lately?" Carly asked her.

Kandy nodded. "Quite a bit, actually. And you?"

"Every day this past week. I did a gang bang scene just this morning with six guys. Now I feel all worn out, and I really wanted to enjoy this party."

Kandy smiled. "I'm sure you'll warm up to it. Maybe just settle for one or two guys rather than six. Or play with a woman or two."

"Are you offering?" Carly said and placed a hand on Kandy's ass.

Kandy kissed the other woman on the lips. "Maybe later."

After mingling and chatting to others in the pool, she got out and felt many eyes on her immaculate butt as she transferred herself to the warm spa. There she squeezed into a space between two hunky guys she'd never seen before and let the bubbles caress her body. As the spa was quite crowded, the guys were hemmed in close to her and their muscular bodies were touching hers. This sent shivers of excitement through her and her sexual desire increased by the minute.

Food and drinks circulated the pool area and Kandy helped herself to a snack and another glass of champagne. She felt like a smoke to go with her drink, but they were still up on the deck. Oh well. Later.

The man on her left was paying her particular attention. He kept looking sideways at her and decided to strike up a conversation with her.

"I know you," he said. "You're Kandy Kane. You're getting pretty famous in the industry."

Kandy smiled at him. He had nice green eyes, friendly and a little bit cheeky.

"I'm sorry, but I don't recognize you at all," she said. "Are you an actor?"

He nodded. "Just starting out." He held out a hand above the turbulent water. "My name's Dan." Kandy shook it. "I love your work. I think I've seen nearly all your films. You are a fantastic porn actress."

"Why, thank you. I aim to please."

"You sure look like you do that," he was adamant. "I'm jealous of the men who get to work with you."

Kandy sipped her drink. She placed a hand between his legs and felt his cock through the lycra of his brief swimwear.

"Nice package," she said. "You'll probably get to work with me one day soon." She put her mouth close to his ear. "I could always test run you tonight."

His cock was beginning to expand down there under the

water and Kandy felt her blood start to simmer. Lust was quickly snaring her in its grip.

"I think I'd really like that," he replied.

There was some action starting to happen over in the pool. Two guys were sitting naked on the edge while a couple of porn stars went down on their mammoth cocks. Up above the pool on the deck, a couple were fucking in one of the reclining chairs.

She said to Dan, "Let's go up and find ourselves a nice comfortable seat."

Together they exited the spa and Kandy led they way to the deck chair where she'd left her towel, dress, shoes and handbag. Dan located his own towel and joined her. She caught him studying the outline of her cunt through the material of her wet G-string.

"Like what you see?" she asked.

He nodded and then apologized.

"No need to apologize," she assured him. "If I didn't like being looked at then I wouldn't be in the porn industry."

"Good point."

Kandy eyed off his package. "Shall we get naked?"

She watched as Dan slipped off his briefs and his sizeable cock sprang to life with anticipation. Kandy removed her top, then the bottoms.

The pair didn't muck around. Straight away they assumed a sixty-niner on the deck chair, with Dan on the bottom. He tongued her throbbing pussy furiously as she swallowed virtually his entire length. With a rapid hand movement she jerked him off between sucks. Dan thrust a finger into her asshole while his tongue was busy inside her cunt.

"That feels really good," she said and let him go on for a minute longer. She then said, "I need this big dick in me." She contemplated riding him, but decided against it. If he wanted to work with her then she wanted to know just how well he could fuck. "Hop up and do me missionary on the chair. Show me what you've got."

He grinned. "Pressure's on."

Kandy got comfortable on her back and spread her legs wide apart. Dan straddled the chair, feet on the deck, and guided his eager cock into her waiting tunnel. Kandy gasped as he thrust hard into her, filling her completely. He sure did have a nice cock.

"Now fuck me," she told him. "If you make me come, I'll tell my manager to organize a scene together."

"Awesome."

Dan went hard and really gave it to her good. Kandy could barely lay still, her body was filled with that much sexual tension. This man could really fuck. His face was a picture of concentration and she enjoyed watching his muscles ripple as he thrust into her endlessly. His heavy balls swayed and slapped against her ass on every penetration. He was going to make her come and come hard.

Kandy clutched the edges of the chair so tightly she thought she was going to snap something. She held her breath, then let it out in a long wail that never seemed to end. Her pussy flooded as Dan continued to ram that big, fat cock into it. She shuddered, shook a couple of times and gasped some more before her orgasm finally began to subside. Dan slowed his pace until he was stroking her gently. He was smiling down at her.

"Did I pass?" he asked.

"With flying colors. That orgasm was magic." She pushed him off her. "I'll talk to Derek, my manager. Now, go do the rounds and enjoy yourself."

Dan shot her another smile and a wink, then went in search of some more action.

Kandy relaxed for a bit, sipping on another drink and smoking a couple of cigarettes. Glancing around she noticed that sex was happening everywhere now. One of the directors she often worked with spotted her and swaggered on over. He was dressed only in shorts and was carrying what looked like a bourbon and Coke.

"Hi, Kandy," he said and kissed her on the lips. He'd done her in the past, on several occasions; one time right after she'd just finished a scene.

"Hi, Bob. No action for you yet?"

He eyed her nakedness. "No, not yet. Just pacing myself."

They chatted while Kandy smoked another cigarette, then she decided to kiss him. One of his hands immediately went to her cunt, where he fingered her wetness. Kandy, meanwhile, had a hold of his hardening cock through his shorts.

"Do you mind?" he asked politely.

She shook her head.

Dan got up and stripped naked, then stood in front of her so she could give him head. No sooner had she started sucking his dick when she was aware of another presence close by. Out of the corner of her eye she saw Jack standing there naked, his cock proudly at attention. She grabbed hold of it and wanked it while continuing to pleasure Bob with her mouth. She switched after a few minutes and rammed Jack's dick deep down her throat while stroking Bob in her left hand. Her pussy was aching to be filled again.

"Who wants to fuck me?" she asked.

"I do," they both said in unison.

Kandy grinned. "Bob was here first."

With Jack laying prone in the chair, Kandy stood on the ground and gave him head while Bob entered her from the rear. Every now and then he would withdraw from her cunt and plunge his cock deep into her ass for a few strokes before returning it to her pussy. This went on for ten minutes, then the guys exchanged places.

While Jack hammered her from the rear, Kandy worked hard on Bob's cock and soon had him squirting inside her mouth. Some of it managed to slide down her throat and she let the remainder dribble down the sides of his shaft. With his balls empty for now, Bob left the scene, only to be replaced by Carly.

The girl sat in front of Kandy and spread her legs. She eyed Kandy expectantly and Kandy obliged by running her tongue up and down the girl's wet slit.

Meanwhile jack was still nailing her from behind and once more she could feel herself approaching a much-needed climax. His cock felt magnificent. No wonder she loved doing scenes with him so much. With Kandy's desire building, Carly's cunt copped a real tongue lashing as Kandy feasted on it like it was her last meal on earth. She came the same time Kandy did and both girls were wriggling and moaning and gasping simultaneously.

Kandy took a break then and smoked a cigarette, where she watched Jack slide into Carly and fuck her hard into the chair. The piece of furniture creaked and groaned under the stress and very soon Carly was exploding a second time. Right after she was done, Jack pulled out of her and shot his thick load all over her breasts. Carly rubbed it into her flesh and giggled.

A little later in the evening Kandy experienced some double penetration from two men she'd never met before. There had been no preceding conversation, not introductions. She didn't know their names or what they did, whether they were actors, crew, or friends of friends. And she didn't care. The pleasure they imparted to her ass and pussy at the same time was all she desired.

The guy underneath her was deep in her pussy, and as she humped him, the man behind her fucked her hard in the ass.

Within minutes she was in the clutches of yet another intense climax that left her breathless. The men didn't let up on her, though. They kept on fucking her until one unloaded in her ass and the other her soaking cunt. Only when they'd both spent their loads did they leave her be.

Kandy lay spread-eagled on the lawn, oblivious to ants or any other critters that may be crawling among the blades. She was exhausted. She knew the night was a long way from over, but right now she was well and truly fucked!

Temptation

It was early Sunday evening as nineteen year old Cale rode his motorbike to his friend's house. The sun had just set behind the mountains in the west, leaving the sky a deep shade of twilight blue. The bike's headlights illuminated the way and he slowed to pull into a driveway.

The first thing he noticed was that Ethan's car wasn't there. His friend always parked it under a tree in the front yard, as his mother's car occupied the single garage. Cale stopped the bike anyway and killed the engine. Removing his helmet and then his gloves, he stuffed the gloves inside the helmet and hung it on one of the mirrors. At the front door he knocked and waited patiently for an answer. None was forthcoming so he knocked again, a little louder this time.

The door suddenly swung open and Ethan's mother, Heather, stood there in a black silk bathrobe tied at the waist. She leaned against the door frame and eyed him up, a smoldering cigarette dangling from the fingers of her right hand.

"Hi, Cale," she said in a friendly voice.

"Hi." Cale felt a little awkward with his best friend's mother wearing nothing but a robe, and he found himself wondering if she had anything on underneath. She was quite an attractive and sexy woman in her very early forties. Her dark hair accentuated the pale skin of her face and she had very nice hips, butt and boobs in Cale's opinion. He'd always secretly fancied her a bit. He cleared his throat. "Is Ethan home?"

"Sorry," she said and took a long drag on her smoke. "He went out a while ago. Went to his girlfriend's place for dinner."

Cale was confused. "I didn't know he had a girlfriend."

Heather shrugged and stepped aside so Cale could enter the house. He walked through a cloud of smoke and down the hall into the tidy living room. There he perched himself on the edge of the couch. Heather picked up an ashtray and seated herself in a chair just to the side of Cale.

"I don't know if she's his girlfriend," she explained. "Ethan only met her last week. Probably just someone he wants to bonk. You know what he's like." She fixed him with her big brown eyes. "Have you found yourself a nice little lady yet?" Cale shook his head. "That's a shame. Gets a bit lonely on your own. I've been single for more than two years now since Ethan's father up and left. Haven't been with a man since...in any way, shape or form."

Cale wasn't sure what to say to that last statement, so he chose not to respond.

Heather stabbed out her cigarette and sprang to her feet. "I feel like a drink. You want to have a drink with me, Cale? Stay for a while. Keep me company."

"I rode my bike here," he said uncertainly.

"One drink won't hurt."

Without waiting for an answer she disappeared into the kitchen, returning a moment later with two glasses. Cale took the glass she offered him and sniffed its contents.

"Brandy," she said and sipped from her own glass. "Really hits the spot."

Cale slipped out of his riding jacket. If he was going to stay a while he wanted to be comfortable. He placed it on the arm of the lounge and tilted some brandy to his lips. It seared his throat on the way down, but it felt good. Heather lit another smoke, shifted her position on the chair and crossed her legs. Cale had been watching her and he was sure he'd just got a glimpse of bare pussy as her legs briefly parted. He took a deep breath and hid his face in his glass, feeling himself start to blush.

"You're a very good looking boy," Heather said to him. "And a nice kid. I've always liked you." She puffed on her smoke and stared at him, exhaling in his direction. "Do you think I'm attractive?"

The question caught him completely off guard and he stammered out a reply. "S...sure. Why not? I know you're a lot older than me, but I think you're very attractive."

She smiled, warmth in her eyes. "Not too much emphasis on the *lot older* part, thank you."

"I didn't mean you're old," Cale said quickly. "Just older than me."

"It's okay," she assured him and sat there for a moment content to sip her drink and puff on her smoke. Her eyes then fixated on Cale again and a strange smile curled the corners of her lovely mouth. "What did you see before?" she asked him.

"See?" He shrugged and shook his head, hoping she wasn't talking about what he thought she might be talking about. "What do you mean?"

"When I crossed my legs before. What did you see?" Again he shook his head and her smile broadened. "I saw you looking down at my crotch. You got a glimpse of my pussy, didn't you?"

"I'm really sorry," he said, feeling a touch panicked. "I didn't mean to. Honest."

"Hush," Heather crooned. "It's perfectly okay. I don't mind one bit. Did you like what you saw?"

He shrugged. "I barely saw anything."

"Would you like to see more?"

Without waiting for an answer Heather untied the robe and pulled the flaps open, revealing her luscious breasts. The older woman then uncrossed her legs and parted them a little so he could see what was on offer down below. Cale felt as if he should look away, but he couldn't. It was like he no longer had control of his eyeballs. Ethan's Mum was gorgeous. Her pussy was completely smooth. Not one hair. And it appeared to be flowering, as if she was aroused.

He cleared his throat again and sipped his brandy, finally managing to peel his eyes away from her seductive and erotic form. He so shouldn't have been admiring her nakedness just now. This was Ethan's mother after all. She was old enough to be *his* mother.

"You haven't told me what you think," Heather pointed out.

He chanced another quick glance and immediately felt his cock start to uncoil in his pants.

"Like I told you, you're gorgeous."

"You didn't use that word before." She leaned forward in her seat. "You're a young man now. You have no girlfriend, but you have needs just like I do. You must be horny. We're both consenting adults. No one has to know. Not Ethan. Not anybody." She whispered the next words conspiratorially. "It can be our little secret."

"I don't know," Cale heard himself say and couldn't believe he wasn't just giving her a flat out NO! She was right; he *was* horny as hell, and right at this moment she was the sole focus of his sexual desire.

"You interrupted me when you knocked at the door before," she told him. "I was in the bedroom, naked and playing with my vibrator."

Cale had been sipping his drink when she spoke the words and he very nearly choked on the alcohol. He coughed and spluttered and could feel his face turning red. Heather got out of her chair and sat beside him on the lounge, where she proceeded to slap him on the back until his coughing fit was under control. Before he could even attempt to resist, her lips were upon his and her tongue was active as it darted in and out of his mouth. He decided he really didn't want to resist and eagerly tongued her back, an action that made his cock swell to a full erection. Heather's hand searched out that throbbing prize and she squeezed it hard through his pants.

When she broke the kiss, she said, "Put your hand between my legs and feel how wet my cunt is."

Cale felt like he was in a dream as he fingered her soaking wet pussy. His mouth started to salivate and he wanted to eat it. Without a word he knelt on the floor, pushed Heather's legs wide apart and started kissing and licking her sweet pussy.

"Oh...yeah!" Heather gasped and placed her hands on his head, encouraging him to feed on her more deeply.

I really shouldn't be doing this, he thought as he dined on her succulent hot flesh. But right now I really don't care. What did it matter anyway? He was having sex with an older woman. No stigma attached to that in the modern world. It was only the fact that it was Ethan's mother that filled him with guilt. If she was just some random cougar coming onto him he wouldn't be thinking anything other than having a great time with her.

He drank from her pussy and swallowed. With his tongue flicking inside her passage, Heather started to moan quite loudly as she rocked her hips back and forth on his face. All he could think about while going down on her was how great it would feel to slide his cock deep inside her.

"You're pretty good at that, Cale," she whispered and moaned some more.

Cale probed her cunt with two of his fingers as he spent

some time giving her clitoris attention. He gently bit it, sucked it and nibbled on it, occasionally running circles around the erogenous nub with his tongue. She tasted so damned good. He couldn't get enough of her tender juices.

Suddenly Heather let out a squeal and her body was rocked by shivers and shudders. Cale smiled into her mound when he realized she was experiencing a climax. It really fed his ego to know that he'd been able to make this older and far more experienced woman come on his face.

"Now it's your turn," she said sweetly and patted the lounge. "You deserve a reward for your efforts." Looking forward to what she was about to do, Cale quickly got into position on the lounge beside her. Heather just looked at him, smiling. She said. "Haven't you forgotten something?"

The realization struck him then. He was so caught up in his world of lust that he hadn't remembered he was still fully clothed. Turning his back to her, Cale stripped off.

"Nice butt," Heather commented. "Now turn around and let me see your cock."

With his dick standing at full attention, Cale slowly turned to face her and Heather's eyes immediately fell below his waistline.

"Mmm. You're quite big." She patted the lounge again. "Come and sit down and I'll suck it for you."

"Can't wait," he quipped and got comfortable.

Heather said, "Neither can I."

Immediately she took his long and throbbing member into her warm mouth and commenced sucking it really hard, working it deep down her throat with the aid of her pumping hand. Cale couldn't help but moan and he wanted her to hear just how good she was making him feel.

Her tongue ran the length of his shaft then until she arrived at his balls. These she sucked on one by one, lapping at them with her tongue at the same time. Once more her wet and slippery tongue was on the move, right up to the tip of his dick where she sampled a drop of pre cum. Now his cock was sliding deep down her throat again. Cale closed his eyes and sighed with pleasure, loving every second of her sensuous blow job.

While he sat there having his dick lovingly sucked by this super sexy older woman, he continually fantasized about fucking her from all different angles and found he couldn't wait to get to that stage of proceedings. When he voiced his urges for penetration, Heather signalled him to be patient a little longer by holding up the palm of her hand.

She sucked noisily now, obviously loving her work. Her head bobbed up and down enthusiastically, repeatedly thrusting his cock into her mouth and down her throat.

"That feels amazing," Cale managed to say.

He opened his eyes and watched her. What a visual it was, watching his cock disappear between her luscious lips and knowing she was really enjoying it as much as he was. He bucked his hips, fucking her mouth. Heather grabbed hold of his balls and scratched them with her nails. Cale kept thrusting into her lips as her tongue lashed the head of his dick.

"Please ride me," he begged. "I need to be in you."

Heather stopped sucking and looked up at him. A smile split her face.

"Okay," she said.

Turning her back to him, the woman straddled his hips with her feet planted on the floor. While she propped herself up with one hand on his chest, she used the other to guide his desperately horny cock into her hot cunt. With one hard thrust she drove his length all the way inside.

"Fuck that feels good," he groaned, loving the feel of her snug wetness engulfing every bit of his cock. He felt himself throb deep inside her as Heather commenced slowly stroking up and down. Grabbing chunks of her hot ass, Cale squeezed her cheeks and helped thrust her down upon himself. Her delectable pussy got wetter and wetter with every stroke. She reached between her legs and stimulated his sensitive ball sack by lightly running her fingertips all over it.

"I can feel them swirling around in there," she told him. "I love that."

"I really want you to come on my cock," he said adamantly.

"Don't worry. I'm sure I will."

A few minutes later, after increasing the tempo of her stroke play, Heather was doing just that. Juice flooded her cunt when she came and washed over his balls in a delicious wave. The

145

woman shivered a few times, then stopped thrusting. She rested just a moment, sucking in deep breaths of air.

"Do me doggie," she decided. "It's one of my favorites."

She got into position by standing on the floor and placing her hands against the backrest of the couch. Cale readily got in behind her and entered her from the rear, immediately thrusting into her hard and deep.

It felt good to be doing some of the work now. As much as he loved sitting back relaxing and being sucked and fucked, a guy really enjoyed putting the physical effort into sex and right now he was in his element. Holding her firmly by the hips, Cale drove his length into her relentlessly, filling her passage with his fat cock and causing her to squeal with every penetration.

"Give it to me," Heather urged him. Cale bucked like a wild bull, slamming his pelvis up against her ass. "That's the way. You're a good lover, Cale."

Cale plundered her pussy from the rear for a good ten minutes. Sweat was starting to bead on his brow and he was puffing hard. He took it slowly for a while, content to watch his cock disappear inside her while giving her the full benefit of his generous length.

"Young cocks are the best," Heather stated. "Fuck me hard again and make me orgasm."

She certainly has no problems coming, Cale thought when Heather was lost in the ecstatic clutches of her third climax.

Next she sat on the padded arm of the lounge while Cale

entered her in some semblance of the missionary position. She ran her lovely hands all over his chest as he fucked her. His loose balls slapped against the cheeks of her ass with every deep penetration, and every so often she would put a hand between her thighs to either stroke her clitoris, or feel his shaft disappearing inside her hot, wet cunt. Her eyes were open and she was staring at his face the entire time he pleasured her in this position.

"Kiss me," she said, her eyes filled with lust.

Cale leaned forward and latched onto her mouth, loving the sensation of their wet lips and tongues rubbing against each other. While they pashed he continued to stroke into her slowly, but rhythmically, grinding the head of his dick into the very end of her lush tunnel. His tongue lashed hers and she sucked on it, draining the juices from it. Cale returned the favor and sucked on Heather's yummy tongue. He ceased kissing her then and concentrated on bringing her to a fourth orgasm. Once he was into a pacy rhythm it didn't take too long at all.

"Here I go again," she said and let out a howl as her body started to shake.

Cale slammed his big dick into her sodden passage, stretching her pussy lips wide apart around his girth. Her beautiful tits bounced around as he rocked her back and forth on the lounge arm. Still her body quivered and shivered as the climax sent wave after wave of pure pleasure through her. Her eyes locked on his again and she finished with a gasp and a very

147

satisfied grin.

"I think it's your turn now," she told him. "Get comfortable on the couch and I'll make you come with my hand." When he was ready, she knelt on the floor, spat in her hand and started wanking his cock. "I wanna watch it all fly out."

Cale was more than excited by the prospect of putting on a show for her. In no time faint tingles started to fill his groin area. He was breathing hard now, the tension building rapidly. His cock throbbed a few times, then started to squirt hot wads of cum high into the air, where they splashed down onto his chest and stomach. When he was finished, Heather ran her tongue through his juice, lapping it up bit by bit and swallowing it all.

He now couldn't wipe the smile off his face. It was the most fun he'd ever had.

One thing was for certain, though. There was no way on earth he was ever going to tell Ethan about this.

Penetrate Me

T hey were in the third venue of five on an organized pub crawl and Brett was feeling half drunk. He was on vacation with his best friend Joe, and they'd been approached in the street earlier to buy tickets for this party night out. So here they were, currently in some dinghy club in the middle of the city. The place looked like it hadn't been renovated in thirty years and its decor was not only dated, but literally starting to crumble apart.

Comprising roughly fifty people, mostly tourists, the group was currently split up with more than half of the patrons out on the dance floor, while the rest hovered near the long bar. Apart from the pub crawl group, hardly anyone else was in the place. And Brett wasn't really surprised.

"I hope the next place is better," Brett said to Joe, who stood beside him drinking a beer while watching the girls dance out on the floor.

Joe nodded. "This place wouldn't be hard to top." He held up his beer. "Just glad we got a free drink on entry."

Brett sipped his own beer, deciding to drink it slowly. While he wanted to have a good time, he didn't want to get hammered only halfway through the night. It was time to pace himself. Besides, he was hoping he might get lucky on this pub crawl. If he was too drunk he wouldn't be able to perform if all went to plan.

They moved away from the bar and stood right at the edge of the sunken dance floor, with its bright colored lights blinking through translucent tiles. Looked like something out of *Saturday Night Fever*; that old disco movie from the seventies. Brett had seen it on TV once and found it totally boring.

He happened to catch the eye of a petite little brunette who was dancing alone. She wore a black dress that barely covered the cheeks of her pert and peachy ass. It was a nice ass and she certainly knew how to move it. The girl edged a little closer to where the friends stood and appeared to be putting on a show for them specifically.

"Makes you feel like biting it, doesn't it?" Joe commented.

"Biting what?"

"Her hot ass. Look at it. Have you ever seen one better?"

The girl turned around, locked eyes with Brett and smiled. Her eyes were dark brown, her teeth white and bright in a pretty face. Her straight hair went halfway down her back and gleamed under the lights. Threatening to burst free of the front of her dress, which was low cut around the cleavage, two delicious looking breasts bulged invitingly against the material.

"I feel like biting those," Brett said to Joe. "Have you ever seen better looking tits than those babies?"

"No, can't say that I have," Joe agreed and sipped his beer. "I think she fancies you a little bit. Wonder if she's got a friend."

"I haven't seen her with anyone. She might be here alone."

"She's a part of the pub crawl, though, isn't she?"

"Yeah. I saw her on the bus before."

The girl moved away then and melded back into the crowd.

Brett managed to nurse the one beer the entire time they were in the old club. Thankfully they didn't have to endure the place for all that long and an announcement was made to exit and board the bus again.

Keen to escape the place, Brett was the first one out the door. He stood beside the bus waiting to be let on board. Joe came up behind him and was followed by a trail of revellers in various states of inebriation. Amid the group was the brunette that had been giving Brett heat in the club before.

The door to the bus opened and one of the organizers indicated it was okay to board. Brett and Joe went right to the back and took up a seat by the rear window. They sat and watched the others file aboard. Many seemed to want seats near the front, but the brunette made her way straight to the rear and sat in a seat right in front of Brett and Joe. She leaned her back against the window and put her legs up on the seat so no one could sit beside her.

The bus rumbled to life and got underway, en route to the fourth venue on the agenda. Brett sure hoped it was a lot more stylish and up to date than that last place. On the short journey he contemplated chatting to the girl, but she seemed more intent on playing around with her iPhone than talking. He decided to leave it for now, see if she gave him any interest at the next club.

Thankfully the trip didn't take very long and soon the bus was pulling to a squeaky halt and everyone hurried off. Needless to say Brett and Joe were last to alight, following right behind the brunette as they entered the doors to the night club.

Inside the place was modern and gleaming, and much busier than the last venue had been. There were two bars on either side, an area to relax in with comfortable red lounges, and a spacious dance floor down the back near the DJ booth.

As they'd come in they'd each been handed a voucher for a free drink at the bar. Joe took Brett's ticket from him.

"Another beer?" he asked.

Brett nodded. "Sure."

It took a few minutes to get served as the nearest bar was quite busy. Joe eventually managed to score a pair of beers and returned to Brett. Armed with fresh drinks, they made their way down to the dance floor, which was packed with females. There were a few guys interspersed among them, hoping to get the chance to move on some of the girls, but it was mostly women.

Brett scanned the dance floor for the brunette. He couldn't see her anywhere. Maybe he should have taken the chance and spoken to her on the bus. It had been a perfect opportunity to strike up a conversation. He guessed he'd been waiting for the invitation and it had never come.

As if somehow reading his thoughts, Joe said, "Why didn't you chat up that girl on the ride over? She was keen on you back at that last dump we were in."

Brett just shrugged and drank some beer.

"He who procrastinates masturbates," Joe added rather sardonically.

"I get the point," Brett assured him. "Anyway, you can't talk. You haven't chatted to anyone either."

"But you had an obvious come on."

"Not on the bus I didn't"

Joe sipped his beer. "I wouldn't have let that bother me. She was probably just trying to play a little harder to get."

Brett shrugged again. Whatever will be will be, he thought.

He spotted her then, coming away from the smaller bar near the dance floor. She saw him, held his gaze for a moment, then glanced out over the dancers. She was definitely on her own, otherwise she would have been sitting with a friend on the bus. Was kind of unusual to come along to things like a pub crawl by yourself.

There was a railing circling much of the dance floor and the brunette leaned her elbows on it as she watched the action. Every so often she glanced in Brett and Joe's direction. The third time she did this she smiled.

Joe nudged Brett and said, "I think she's keen again. Now's your chance. Go for it."

Brett nodded. It seemed to him that she'd been checking them both out on this occasion. Still, time to get to work. He wasn't going to get laid by talking to nobody.

"Hi," he said as his opening line, and internally patted himself on the back for being so witty.

The brunette turned and smiled. "Hi," she replied in a soft, slightly husky voice, then sipped her drink through a straw. Brett liked that huskiness in her tone.

"My name's Brett."

"I'm Tina." She held out her hand and Brett shook it.

"Are you on your own tonight?"

She nodded. "I often come out on my own."

"So you're a local then, not a tourist?"

"Yeah, I live here. You?"

Brett nodded towards Joe. "My friend and I are on holiday. We thought this pub crawl might be a good way to meet some people."

She grinned. "And now you have." She looked towards Joe. "Tell your friend to come over. The more the merrier, as they say."

Brett got Joe's attention and waved him over. He casually strolled across the carpet and joined them.

"I'm Joe," he said and offered her his best smile.

"Tina," she said and shook his hand. She studied Joe a moment, then Brett. "You're both quite good looking. Just my type." She sipped her drink and gave each of them the full body scan with her brown eyes.

What was this girl's story? Brett wondered. Who was she interested in?

154

The three made small talk for a few minutes until everyone was out of drinks. While Joe went to the bar to fetch another round, Tina made a candid confession to Brett which stunned him.

"I have a fetish," she said, locking eyes with Brett's. "I love my sex, but one man is not enough to satisfy my needs."

For a moment Brett couldn't find his tongue. When he did manage to finally reply, his voice came out more like a croak. "What are you saying? That you want both of us?"

Tina smiled. "You catch on quick. That's exactly what I'm saying."

"Like, sexually? Tonight?"

Tina nodded. "You look a little shocked." Brett just shrugged. "I am what I am, and I'm not ashamed of how I am or fulfilling my desires." She glanced over toward the bar, where Joe was still waiting to be served. "Have you and your friend never done a woman together?"

"No," Brett said quickly, not too sure if that prospect interested him at all. He wasn't selfish, but wasn't used to sharing in that way. He pondered it for a moment. It wasn't just himself either. He wasn't sure what Joe would think of that idea.

Joe was now making his way back with drinks. He handed another vodka to Tina and a beer to Brett. The three said cheers and drank up. Both Brett and Tina were looking at Joe and Joe noticed.

"What?" he said.

Brett answered, "Tina has a proposal for you. Well, for us."

Tina was candid. "I was just telling Brett that I enjoy having two men."

"In bed?" Joe blurted out.

"Yes." Tina seemed to get a little flustered then. "Look. I don't want to waste your time or mine. I have needs, and I want to satisfy them tonight. Are you two interested or not?"

Brett and Joe looked at one another. Brett had already decided he would give it a go. It was now in Joe's hands.

Joe said, "Sure. Why not?"

Tina looked at Brett.

"I'm in," he said.

This brought a huge smile to Tina's face. "Then drink up, boys. There's work to be done...but the fun kind."

They ditched the remainder of the pub crawl and caught a cab back to their inner-city hotel. The elevator dropped them off on the tenth floor, where they padded down a carpeted hallway and entered their room.

"I'm feeling so hot right now," Tina said and immediately started to disrobe.

She certainly isn't shy, Brett thought as he and Joe pushed the suite's two double beds together. By the time they had done this Tina was already naked.

Both guys eyed her shapely and hot little body with pure lust. She was certainly built for sex, with that gorgeous ass, big boobs and curvy hips. Her pussy was waxed smooth, the lips slightly parted as she was already aroused.

She climbed onto the beds and positioned herself in the middle. Brett jumped aboard and immediately started feasting on those bountiful breasts while Joe parted her legs and busied himself tasting her pussy.

Brett tried to put it out of his mind that there were three of them involved and just enjoyed what he was doing. Tina's tits were awesome to suck, with big brown nipples that stiffened into mini temples. She was gasping softly as the two men pleasured various parts of her body simultaneously. Brett had the urge to kiss her, so he nibbled his way up her throat and latched onto her eager mouth. Tina's tongue darted into his and they kissed furiously. Brett loved lots of tongue when kissing and Tina gave him plenty. His cock had reached full hardness inside his pants and he decided it was time to let it out. He couldn't wait for this uninhibited and horny girl to suck it.

He got off the bed and stripped naked. Joe was too intent feeding on her mound to bother getting naked yet. He would when he was ready. Tina eyed Brett's cock with lust and indicated for him to bring it to her. Back on the bed on his knees, he edged over to her until he was within range of her mouth, where she engulfed his throbbing rod and readily took most of it down her throat.

Joe looked up from her pussy and watched as Tina gave Brett fantastic head. Brett felt a tinge of self-consciousness then, but tried to ignore it. He was determined to have a great time.

A few minutes later Joe got up and shed his clothes. Back on the bed he knelt between the girl's outstretched legs and guided his cock into her cunt. She spat Brett out as Joe penetrated her fully and gasped with absolute pleasure.

"How's her pussy feel?" Brett quizzed his friend as Tina resumed sucking his dick.

"Awesome," Joe reported. "Really wet and quite tight. You're gonna love it." He grinned as he stroked her. "If I ever let you have a turn."

Tina spat out Brett's cock a second time and said adamantly, "You will. I want both of you to fuck me senseless, not just one of you."

"Looks like you've been told," Brett said to his mate. He groaned as Tina deep-throated him again and watched as those lush lips of hers worked away on his member. She had a beautiful mouth and he couldn't wait to feel himself buried deep inside her hot cunt. He got that chance a few minutes later.

"Let's swap now," Tina said. She looked at Brett. "I want you to do me doggie while I suck Joe's cock."

The three quickly got into position. Joe leaned his back against the wall at the head of the bed and Tina wasted no time taking his dick down her throat. Meanwhile, Brett probed the entrance to her tunnel with the head of his cock, then plunged into her depths with one aggressive thrust of his hips and buttocks. She groaned when he reached the end of her passage and started thumping into her from the rear. Joe was right, she

158

was quite tight...and extremely wet. Her pussy was also generating a lot of heat. This girl was on fire.

Determined to give her a damned good fucking, Brett gave it everything he had, driving his cock into her depths with relentless vigor. He wanted to make her come and he wasn't about to let up until she did.

He got his wish in a matter of minutes. As the climax rocked her body, Tina removed Joe's length from her mouth and howled in ecstasy as her figure shook and trembled. When it had abated she requested they switch again. Now Joe had her from behind while Brett sat at the head of the bed and had his cock gobbled up like a delicious sweet.

This girl sure knew how to give a great blow job and had obviously had plenty of practice perfecting her oral talents. Brett felt like he could sit there all night and have her suck him off.

Joe was going hell for leather on her pussy, presumably not wanting to be outdone by his mate.

"Make her come all over your cock," Brett encouraged him.

"I plan to," he grunted as his body slapped against the young woman's peachy ass cheeks. His actions were making her rock back and forth so wildly that she was having trouble keeping Brett's dick in her mouth.

"I'm gonna come again," she announced and started howling once again. Trembles rippled through her body. She squeezed Brett's cock very tightly in her hand as she went through the pleasurable sensations that only an orgasm could give someone.

She rode Brett next while Joe stood on the bed beside her so she could taste his cock. Brett helped her out by thrusting into her from below, intermittently playing with those big, bouncing breasts. They were by far and away the best tits he'd ever laid his hands on. Her pussy was still drenched with juice and he could feel it coating his balls. Her lips kissed his sack with every downward stroke and it felt awesome.

Joe had a hold of the sides of her face now and was thrusting his cock in and out of her mouth. Brett had the random thought then that Tina must be getting a sore jaw by now. If she was it didn't seem to bother her. She was greedily taking his length down her throat.

One of her hands reached behind her then and she massaged his balls with her fingertips, feeling his wet shaft every time she rose up it. Brett slapped her ass a few times, then her titties. Her thrusting increased in urgency. She withdrew Joe's dick from her throat and let out a long groan as she came for the third time. This orgasm didn't last as long as the last two, and soon she was ready for another position change.

Joe got in behind her as the pair lay on the bed and spooned her. Brett positioned himself near her mouth again so once more she could feed on his cock. Joe gave it to her slowly and sensually and Tina mirrored that in the way she gave Brett head. She was now licking and sucking his cock rather lovingly, and much more gently than before. Brett quite enjoyed this new style. She spent some time licking and kissing his balls, an action that sent tingles of pleasure all through his body. He felt like his head was swimming with desire and he still couldn't quite believe that he and his best mate were here in the room together giving it to this hot and randy chick.

Brett took a turn spooning her next. Tina gave her mouth a rest and just slowly stroked Joe's cock with her hand as Brett fucked her from behind. The different angle their spooning bodies created felt great, and her pussy massaged the head of his dick in a unique way. He could hear her wet pussy making soft, sucking sounds as he stroked it, and that served to heighten his arousal.

"Give it to me," Tina whispered in that husky, sexy voice of hers. "Build me up slowly to another orgasm."

Brett, not wanting to disappoint, did just that. It took a further ten minutes of slow and methodical stroke play to get her there, but when she finally arrived, it was her longest and most explosive climax of the night so far.

Tina lay there for a while catching her breath. When she'd recovered, she said, "I need DP. One in my ass and one in my pussy."

Brett knew Joe liked a bit of anal with a woman, so he voted Joe have that particular passage while he pleasured her cunt. He wasn't really into anal himself; always considered it a poor substitute when there was a beautiful wet pussy nearby to fuck.

With Joe lying flat on his back, Tina sucked his cock again, got it all nice and wet, then positioned herself above it and

161

guided it into her ass. When it was comfortably inside, she leaned back and spread her legs wide apart. Brett knelt between her thighs, rubbing the head of his cock all over her moist lips.

She looked into Brett's eyes and said, "Penetrate me."

Brett didn't need to be told twice. He plunged into her tunnel and immediately started fucking her vigorously while she squirmed around on top of Joe's cock. He could feel his balls touching Joe's every time he thrust into her, but he tried very hard to ignore that. They weren't doing anything gay, just giving this woman what she needed most.

Having two cocks in her at once was really getting Tina off. She had her eyes closed tight and the look on her face was one of intense pleasure. She climaxed within minutes, and this time her orgasm was so full on that she squirted when she came, spraying fluid all over Brett's groin as he continued to stroke her tunnel with his lengthy cock.

Finally it was time for the guys to have their release. Tina sat on a corner of the bed with Brett and Joe either side of her, taking turns sucking their cocks. While she worked on one with her mouth she would stroke the other in her soft, expert hand. Joe built to a climax first, and when he was about to ejaculate, Tina clamped her mouth firmly over the head of his cock so she didn't waste a drop.

Brett took a little longer to reach his goal, but he now had Tina's full focus. Her mouth plunged down his shaft repeatedly as her tongue worked away on the head. Soon he felt the first stirrings of impending release in his loins. The sensation rapidly increased and he grunted loudly as he finally started to shoot his cum into her waiting mouth. It was such a relief to finally empty his balls and he sighed with contentment.

Suddenly Tina seemed in a great hurry. She quickly put her clothes back on, slipped into her shoes, snatched up her handbag, said a quick, "Thank you," and was out the door, leaving Joe and Brett staring at each other.

Joe shrugged and said, "Well that was different."

Jack Hammer

J ack Hammer is a porn star.

He loved his screen name and the actresses loved working with him. And why wouldn't they? He was extremely good looking, with a well-muscled physique, tanned, had a big cock and certainly knew how to please in the bedroom. Or wherever they happened to be filming at the time.

Jack didn't just get laid on camera. His physical affections were just as in demand off screen. The adult stars were like a family that worked together and played together. On top of that, he was married to adult star and director, Jamelia Whyte.

Right now he was sitting on a couch having almost finished a scene for his latest film. The blonde actress was working his long, thick dick in and out of her mouth, aiding the stimulation by jerking him off with her hand at the same time. They were going for the cum shot and he could feel himself building rapidly toward a dramatic climax.

Right when he was about to explode the actress pulled his cock from her mouth and let it squirt all over his chest and six pack abs. She then proceeded to run her tongue through the sea of warm jizz and smiled for the camera.

"Cut!" Jack's wife called and the cameras stopped rolling. "That was a fantastic scene, guys. Well done." Jamelia then came over and kissed her husband on the lips and stroked her hand through the actress's hair. 'That's going to look great when it's edited and polished up. Good job." She whispered in Jack's ear. "How'd the new girl do?"

"She was really good. I loved every second of it," Jack assured his wife.

Jamelia nodded. "I think that'll really show through on the footage, too."

"So, what's next?" he asked.

"Tonight you have another scene for our new series."

Jack grinned. "Awesome."

The new series was titled - *So You Want to Fuck a Porn Star*. Jack was the only male actor in the series. Real life amateurs were encouraged to send in their details, including professional photos, from which the best of them were picked to star in amateur scenes with Jack. The girls got paid for their efforts and, if they were impressive enough, were offered contracts to join the industry as adult stars. Jamelia was the brainchild behind the idea and Jack loved working in the new series. The women were hot and fresh and real. Generally they had a bit of a thing for him to begin with and were already dying to fuck him. Which made the action that much more realistic and enjoyable when it came to the actual filming of the scenes. Tonight's would be his fifth scene in the series, which would complete the first DVD.

"Babe? My pussy's really wet after watching that scene," Jamelia told him.

Jack nodded his understanding. "Just give me a few minutes to recover and I'll help you out with that."

Jamelia lit two cigarettes and handed one to him. She then fetched an ashtray and sat down on the couch beside him. Together they smoked in silence as the crew packed up the gear and started carting it out of the hotel suite. By the time Jack had finished his smoke he felt like he was ready to give his wife some relief.

"Just a quickie," she said. "You need to save some energy for tonight."

With those words she hitched up her skirt and removed her white silk panties. There was a distinct wet patch in the crotch from where the juice had leaked from her horny cunt. The sight of his wife's needy pussy immediately gave Jack a raging hard-on. He spread Jamelia's legs wide apart and entered her with one powerful thrust.

Stroking in and out with expert rhythm, Jack watched his fat dick split her slippery lips very wide apart. Already she was moaning uncontrollably and he knew it wouldn't take long to make her come.

Jamelia really needed to do more scenes herself, to satisfy her desires. Of late she'd become more focused on directing films rather than playing a role in them. As her husband, Jack satisfied her desires as much as he could, but he was so often working he didn't always have much left for her. Still, there were the parties where she got laid, quite often more than once and by more than one man. Then there were the women, too. She loved sex with women just as much as she loved be well-fucked by randy guys.

He decided she was fine. She had as much of him as he could give, and she had plenty of sex outside of their relationship to keep her high sex drive in check.

Jamelia came a few minutes later. She bucked her hips against him as the waves of ecstasy washed over her.

The crew were still in the process of packing up and were oblivious to the sex happening on the couch. They were used to it and had seen this go on hundreds of times before.

Jack ejaculated for the second time in fifteen minutes when he came inside his wife. He didn't have much left, but gave her everything he had. She seemed more than content with his offering.

The afternoon was spent relaxing by the pool and resting up for tonight's scene. Shooting was going to be done around the pool at Jack and Jamelia's lavish home. The lighting and other equipment had already been set up. It was now just a matter of the crew showing up to do the work. Tonight's amateur guest star was named Gina. Or at least that was the name she wanted to go by.

Jack had a late lunch while Jamelia spent the majority of the afternoon on the phone. After eating he stripped off and dove into the pool, shattering the glassy blue water that shimmered in the late afternoon sunlight. He floated around on his back for a while, staring up at the azure sky. It promised to be fantastic weather for tonight's shoot and he found he couldn't wait to get into it.

He stayed in the water until the sun was almost setting. After toweling himself dry he lit a cigarette and reclined naked on a deck chair, enjoying the cool caress of a light breeze. The smoke was chased down with a shot of tequila from a decanter on an outdoor table. As the warmth of the liquor burned down his throat, Jack immediately poured himself another. He found a couple of shots about an hour before helped fire him up and gave him an edge; especially for night time shoots.

Gina arrived about the same time as the crew. She was ushered into a downstairs bathroom where the makeup artist went to work glamming her up. By now Jack was dressed in brief white swimmers that were barely big enough to contain his more than generous package. He chatted to one of the camera operators as the crew set up for filming. It was dark by now and the pool area was subtly illuminated with lighting placed discreetly and strategically about the area.

Jamelia emerged from the house and kissed her husband on the lips. "You ready, my sweet?"

"Always ready for action," Jack replied with a grin.

"Have fun. Gina's almost ready to join you on set. We'll do the usual interview, then we'll cut to the action. You take the lead with her and I'll let you two know throughout the shoot if I want to capture something in particular."

Jack smoked another cigarette while he awaited Gina's arrival by the pool. Another shot of tequila was downed and by the time Gina came out to face the cameras, Jack was raring to go. He loved fucking the amateurs. Even though they were inexperienced on set, they always showed great enthusiasm. They were carefully screened by himself and Jamelia, so they were always extremely attractive to Jack and had the attitude they were looking for.

Jamelia instructed Gina to recline on one of the many deck chairs in the pool area. Gina was a brunette. Her face had been beautifully made up, her hazel eyes brought out with vivid eye shadow and her lips enhanced with cherry-red lip gloss. All of the makeup was waterproof as some swimming in the pool would be involved in this scene. Gina had been dressed in a white bikini, and she wore a thin white cotton shirt that was left unbuttoned so her curvaceous figure could be seen.

Jack stayed out of the camera shot while Jamelia conducted the brief interview with their amateur actress. Gina appeared very calm and relaxed, as if she'd done this many times before. Jamelia started by asking Gina some mandatory questions, like her name and what she did for a living etcetera.

"So, Gina, what made you want to appear in our film?" Jamelia asked the young would-be actress.

Gina grinned lasciviously. "Well, Jack Hammer is my favorite adult actor. I've seen many of his films and have often fantasized about what it would be like to have sex with him."

"Tonight you get your chance to do just that. How do you feel right now?"

"Very excited and very, very horny."

"Jack has a beautiful body, doesn't he?"

"Yes, and the world's most desirable cock." Gina giggled. "I can't wait to suck it and ride it and come all over it."

"Do you feel nervous about the fact that this is all going to be filmed and put on show for the world to see?"

Gina shook her head. "Not at all. Thinking about that just gets me even more excited."

"Are you hoping for a career in the adult film industry?"

"I'd love to do porn for a living, getting paid to fuck hot men who really know how to please a woman."

"Okay, Gina. That'll wrap it up. Are you ready to get into the action?"

Gina stood up and slipped off the shirt. "Definitely."

The scene started off with Jack and Gina having a swim in the pool. The pair frolicked about in the water having some fun before coming together in a glow of soft lighting to kiss. It started as a few gentle pecks, lips nipping at one another. Gina had her arms wrapped around Jack's neck, while Jack had her firm butt cheeks cupped in his hands underwater. Tongues flicked out and caressed tentatively before plunging into each other's mouths and kissing heatedly.

Jack's cock was already fully erect inside his swimmers and he jammed his erection hard against the young woman's crotch, where he proceeded to grind against her whilst they tongued one another furiously.

Jamelia called out, "Looking good, guys. Very sensual."

"God, I'm so turned on," Gina said as she continued to nip at Jack's lips. She reached a hand underwater and took hold of Jack's throbbing member. "I've often wondered what your dick would feel like to touch. It's magnificent. Can't wait to taste it."

The pair kissed again and Jamelia signaled for a close up of the tongue action.

"Okay," Jamelia called out. "Let's do some oral."

"I get to suck your dick now," Gina whispered with a smile.

Jack sat on the edge of the pool while Gina helped him squirm out of his swimwear, These were tossed onto the deck and Jack sat there with his huge cock proudly displayed for Gina and the cameras to see.

"Wow," Gina said as she knelt in the shallows and studied his magnificent member up close and in real life for the very first time. "I still can't believe I'm actually doing this." She lightly stroked it and ran her fingertips down its long length to his heavy balls. "This is going to be so much fun."

"You can suck it now, Gina," Jamelia directed, a slight smirk on her face. Then, to a cameraman, "Let's get a close up of this."

Gina gripped Jack's cock tightly in her right hand and ran her tongue over the tip. She kissed the head and licked rings around it before opening her mouth wide and swallowing several inches of his shaft. She withdrew with smacking lips and licked down his length to tongue his sack.

Jack felt very relaxed sitting on the edge of the pool, legs spread apart and feet dangling in the cool water. The sensation of Gina's mouth on his manhood was exquisite. Every lick of her velvety tongue and touch of her wet lips sent tingles through him.

As time went on she got more into the blow job and really started to suck him hard, using her hand to pump his shaft down her throat. Every so often she would lick his length and finish by paying attention to his balls. Then his cock would be back in her mouth again. He was nine inches long and Gina managed to swallow at least seven inches on more than one occasion.

This oral action was all carefully captured on camera. Jamelia regularly called for different camera angles, lighting and focal lengths.

"You're great at giving head," Jack complimented Gina as the young actress continued to lovingly and enthusiastically lick, kiss and suck his cock.

She spat on it and vigorously pumped it up and down in her fist. Jack gasped and looked up at the starry sky. He continued to gasp and groan and loved the way every bit of the action was captured on camera. One of his greatest pleasures was watching the scenes he'd performed in once they'd been fully edited and mastered. It was such a turn on seeing himself fucking all these beautiful women. His wife loved watching them back too, as well as the films she starred in herself. There was no jealousy in their marriage. They met through the porn industry and knew exactly what they were getting into when they formed a relationship. There was never any expectation of exclusivity; not with the work they were both involved and heavily entrenched in.

When Gina took his dick back into her mouth, Jack leaned forward, seized a handful of her black hair and jammed her head down onto him relentlessly. On one occasion he held her head down at Jamelia's request, his cock deep down Gina's throat. When he let her up for air, she spat him out and dribbled saliva down her chin. She only rested for a second before greedily sucking his cock back into her mouth.

"Swap positions now," Gina instructed.

Jack dropped into the water and Gina took up a seat on the pool edge. She slipped off her bikini bottom, spread her legs very wide apart and placed her feet on the edge. Her steamy cunt was now beautifully exposed and glistened with pool moisture under the lights. Her snatch was shaved smooth except for a tiny crop of black hair just above her slit. As Jack moved his face between her legs, her heady aroma intoxicated him. Cameras zoomed in and light was focused on her pussy as his tongue probed her lips and slipped into her passage.

"Very sweet," he commented and lashed her erect clitoris with his tongue. He sucked on her lips, then delved into the folds so her flowing juices could coat his tongue once more. Gina was extremely wet and obviously desperate to be fucked. She was going to be a good root, he could tell, and would no doubt put on a great show for the camera crew.

Gina's hand massaged his hair as he ate her out. In all honesty she had one of the freshest and most flavorsome pussies he'd ever had the pleasure of tasting. She raked her nails across his scalp and applied light pressure, encouraging him to lick her more deeply. Jack's tongue strained, reaching into her hole as far as it could stretch. The entire time he performed cunnilingus he was dying to fuck her. It wouldn't be long now before his wife gave the word for penetration. His big cock was throbbing underwater and it was desperate for some pussy action.

Jamelia delayed the call and Jack found himself eating Gina's muff for another five minutes. His tongue was getting sore from over-use and his face was covered in pussy juice. Jamelia finally called for some fucking and Jack took it upon himself to decide the first position. He got out of the pool and reclined in a deck chair. Holding his dick up, he signalled Gina to hop on. Gina straddled him and lowered her hungry cunt down onto the head of his cock. It slipped straight in and slowly inched all the way inside. She paused a moment to absorb the sensation of having her pussy completely filled with her favorite porno star's hot meat.

"You like that cock?" Jack asked her.

"I love this cock," she said. "It's my fantasy cock."

"Fuck it then."

With her feet flat on the ground and her hands resting on

Jack's chest, Gina rose and fell slowly and methodically, taking him all the way in before rising back up to the tip. She was using all nine inches of his length and it felt fantastic.

Jamelia had two camera angles on the scene; one filming the action from behind and the other filming on an angle from the front. A boom mike hovered just out of sight above the actors' heads.

Jack lay there on the deck chair and just took it. Gina's pussy was very wet and quite tight. When he sank all the way in he could feel his cock stretching the extremities of her cunt. She was in no pain, though, just pure pleasure. She reached a hand behind her and played with his balls as she fucked him. Jack could feel juice on them, she was that wet.

"That looks fantastic, guys," Jamelia praised. "Keep going just like that, Gina. Bend forward just a little so we can get full view of your gorgeous pussy riding that enormous dick."

Gina did as asked and leaned forward. Her tits now swayed in front of Jack's face, though they were still clad in the white bikini top. Jack reached around her back and undid the top, then pulled it over her head and tossed it onto the deck. Taking a beautiful boob in each hand, he caressed the nipples to full hardness while Gina continued to pound his cock.

"Fuck it!" he said through clenched teeth. "Come all over it."

He spanked her ass to spur her on. Gina responded with a squeal of pain, but she rode him even faster. In the background Jamelia was grinning, loving Gina's enthusiasm. The cameras

175

were capturing some great action.

Gina came with a cry into the night. Her body shivered and her pussy clenched tighter around Jack's rigid shaft. She gasped for air as she continued to thump her pussy onto his dick. When she was done she kissed Jack passionately.

"Cut!" Jamelia called. "Take five, guys. We'll pick it back up with some doggy action."

Jack relaxed and smoked a cigarette while Gina sipped on a glass of lemonade. Jamelia was busy directing the crew to change some lighting angles and to set up the cameras in different spots. By the time Jack stubbed out his smoke, Jamelia had everything the way she wanted it.

By now Jack had gone flaccid, so Gina spent a few minutes sucking him back to full hardness. She smiled at her handiwork and once again admired his beautiful dick.

Jamelia directed Gina to bend over the deck chair, grasping its sides and poking her ass into the air.

"Do you need any lube?" Jamelia asked her.

"God, no! I'm soaking wet!"

As the cameras started rolling once more, Jack moved in behind her, cock in hand and guided the eager head back into her hole. He thrust into her in one long and very slow stroke, creating good imagery of entry for the nearest camera.

"That looks beautiful," Jamelia commented as she herself moved in for a close-up view of the action. "Fuck her hard, Baby," she whispered to Jack. "This girl's been dying to be

176

fucked by your cock for years. Give her what she's been fantasizing about. Make her scream for the cameras."

Jack lived up to his screen name and gave it to Gina like a jackhammer. She did indeed scream and once more she came and put on a great show.

She was flipped over then and taken in the missionary position. This time Jack took it slowly, with long and deep strokes designed to be a great visual. Which is what it was all about anyway. He pulled his cock out and re-entered her a few times, withdrew it again and used his fingers to spread her cunt lips wide apart so the close-up camera could capture the pink shot. When he sank his member back into her, he didn't take it out again, just kept on fucking her until Jamelia called for reverse cowgirl.

Jack reclined on the chair and Gina straddled him while facing the cameras. She picked up his length, probed her opening with the head, then dropped her weight on his cock and drove it into her depths. Jack cupped her ass cheeks and helped her hump him. As far as watching porn went, in his opinion, reverse cowgirl offered the best visuals of the fucking action.

Gina's pussy was so wet it made delicious sucking sounds as she fucked him. It was so hot inside her and so damned tight, he feared he might come prematurely. Jack forced himself to momentarily think of something else until the tingles of impending release subsided. Once it was under control, he thrust rapidly into her from underneath, making her pant and moan and squeal out of control. In less than a minute she exploded for the third time, squirting a spray of juice from her cunt that brought a gleam to Jamelia's eyes. It was great footage. And best of all, it wasn't staged.

Jamelia allowed Gina a few moments to recover before calling for the money shot. Gina climbed off Jack's cock and knelt on the ground beside him. First she licked her own juices from his shaft, then set to work stimulating the head with her lips and tongue. All the while she pumped his cock with her hand.

Jack lay there, eyes closed, and lapped it up. This was his favorite part of every scene; where he got to relax and let the woman - or women - make him ejaculate. He loved coming on camera, adored putting on a show. He knew all the men watching porn were wishing they were the ones fucking all the hot women he got to fuck for real. Best of all, he was making loads of cash doing it!

Gina would make him come in no time, he knew. She was great at giving head and she had an expert hand with consistent rhythm. After only a few minutes he felt the tingles surge through his loins and the cum shoot up his shaft. The first one squirted high into the air and landed on his chest with a splatter. When the second wad shot from his cock, Gina kept her eyes on it and managed to catch it on her tongue. She quickly swallowed it and caught the next few squirts as well. When he was finished she greedily sucked the cum from off his skin and drank every drop. After that she milked the last drops from his shank and

178

swallowed those too.

"I think we're onto a winner here," Jamelia announced happily and called a halt to the action.

* * *

The next day was a day off. No work...If you could call it that.

Jack took Jamelia to a secluded beach where they could tan, have a swim and just relax and unwind. They'd both been working hard this past month and really needed a day of doing nothing.

It was quite early in the morning when they set off in their silver Mercedes convertible. The sky was clear for the most part, but there were a few clouds about that momentarily hid the sun. Hopefully they didn't get any thicker.

The area of beach they liked to go was half an hour's drive away. The pair smoked a few cigarettes on the way and enjoyed the freedom of the wind in their hair as they drove south along the coast road. Jack pulled off the road and parked the car in the shade of a grove of trees. Wearing only their swimmers, they took towels from the back seat and strolled through the soft sand to the water's edge. The tide was on the way out, but they placed their towels above the high tide line anyway and lay down to soak up some rays.

Jamelia removed her top, leaving her in only a thong bikini bottom. Jack wore skimpy black lycra swimming shorts. He glanced about the beach, looked left and right, saw no one else about.

Just how they liked it.

After a few minutes of sunbaking, with the cloud cover increasing and moving towards the sun, both Jack and Jamelia removed their swimwear completely to get an all-over tan. There was a gentle breeze blowing, which was enough to keep the temperature comfortable.

Jack listened to the pounding of the surf and he found the sound inviting, enticing him in for a swim. He slipped his swimwear back on and stood up, told his wife he was going for a dip and waded into the surf.

The first few waves crashed into his thighs, the fourth smashed across his chest and the next he dove under, emerging on the other side and immediately ducking another breaker. When he broke the surface he flicked water out of his hair and felt exhilarated. The water was cool and verging on cold, but it felt great. Made him feel revitalized and alive. He dove beneath the surface again and swam underwater parallel to the shore. When he came up a wave crashed into the side of his head, stinging his ear. He shook his head to clear it and rubbed at his ear. Turning around he spied a wave coming that he thought he might be able to catch and started swimming onto it. Just as the lip started to break he angled sideways down the face, right arm leading the way, and rode the wave almost all the way into shore. He came to a stop in the shallows and looked up to see Jamelia striding into the water totally naked.

"You have such a hot body," he said to her in admiration as his eyes lustfully roamed over her smooth and flawless, cosmetically-enhanced breasts, and the black pubic hair shaved in the shape of a V pointing the way to her delectable cunt.

"You horny, Babe?" she said and jumped on top of him.

She ground her pussy against his stiffening cock and tongued his hungry mouth. Jack tongued her back and felt his big cock reach full strength inside his brief swimwear. Jamelia sat up and continued to grind her pussy against him. She rocked back and forth, stimulating her clit on his hardness, a soft moan escaping her lips. She closed her eyes and squeezed her big tits together, running her index fingers over her jutting nipples.

"I wanna fuck you," Jack stated the obvious.

She grinned and opened her eyes. "I know you do, Baby, but it looks like we've got company."

Jack tilted his head to the side and very nearly copped a mouthful of salt water. A group of guys and girls were walking along the deserted beach and heading in their direction. Jamelia made no attempt to cover up. And why would she? She was more than used to exposing her body for public viewing. As the group came in line with the two in the shallows, all of them having a good gawk, a knowing look crossed the face of one of the young men.

"Hey!" he said to his friends. "That's those two porn stars! Jack Hammer and Jamelia Whyte."

"Hey! It is too!" exclaimed one of the other guys.

"I wouldn't know a porn star if I tripped over one," said one of the girls.

But another young woman said, "I recognize Jack Hammer. I've seen him in a few films. He's hot!"

Jamelia stared at the group as they paused adjacent to the two porn stars. "Would you like us to put of a free show for you?" she asked the group.

"Sure!" one of the males responded with enthusiasm.

Jamelia moved up Jack's body and planted her pussy right on his face, where he proceeded to lick it and cause Jamelia to moan.

"My husband has a magnificent tongue," she said to the crowd.

"And a magnificent cock," one of the girls retorted.

"You want to see his cock?" asked Jamelia.

All the women nodded.

Jamelia turned around and sat back down on Jack's mouth. She then proceeded to removed his swimmers, exposing his huge dick for the onlookers to see. Jamelia leaned forward and took Jack's cock into her mouth, where she jammed almost the entire length down her throat. Jamelia gorged his cock and Jack gasped from the intensity of her sucking as he continued to lick her horny wet hole. He slid his long tongue deep into her cunt and tasted her spongy walls. Juice trickled into his mouth and ran down his throat. His wife always tasted fantastic and today was no exception.

182

There was clapping from the onlookers when Jamelia managed to swallow all nine inches of Jack's cock.

So much for their deserted beach, Jack mused. But he didn't mind. He and Jamelia were about to fuck anyway before the group came along, and he loved putting on a show.

"When are you going to fuck it?" a female said to Jamelia.

One of the men said, "Yeah. Let's see you ride it."

Jamelia teased the audience and didn't give them what they wanted right away. She licked up and down Jack's shaft and stroked his balls with her fingertips. Jack sucked hard on her cunt and was quite noisy about it.

They were no longer in the shallows, the outgoing tide taking the water line further down.

A few minutes later Jamelia decided to give the audience what they wanted. She moved down Jack's body and hovered above his dick, where she probed her entry with the throbbing head. It pierced her pussy and disappeared inside, followed immediately by his entire thick length. Jamelia gasped and started to moan as she slowly rode up and down.

The crowd gathered around in front of her, one of the boys even getting down low so he could get a good look at Jack's cock splitting Jamelia's luscious cunt apart. Smart phones came out of pockets and photos were taken. Normally Jack and Jamelia charged for that sort of thing, but today they didn't care. If anything, this freebie show might help promote their latest releases and ultimately lead to more DVD and internet subscription sales.

Jamelia's randy cunt was very tight around Jack's shaft. For all the fucking she'd done in her life, she somehow managed to maintain a really tight pussy.

Must be those daily pelvic exercises, he decided.

"Listen to the sound it's making," one of the guys said. "She's so wet."

A girl added, "And why wouldn't she be? Any pussy's going to be wet with that cock fucking it. Mine's wet right now, just quietly."

"Wanna fuck?" the guy asked her hopefully.

"Not now. I'm watching the show. Maybe later."

Jack took his wife doggy next and hammered her with long, deep strokes. The onlookers gathered in close for a good perve, watching closely as jack's nine inch length was continually swallowed up eagerly by Jamelia's hungry pussy.

"I'm gonna come," Jamelia announced a moment before her body shuddered and convulsed and she let out a series of excited gasps. She also uttered a few incoherent words as she came.

"She sounds just like she does on video when she comes," someone noted.

A girl said, "I want to see Jack come."

Jamelia grinned, her orgasm now passed. "All in good time," she promised. "Right now I want to ride my husband some more."

This time she mounted him in the conventional cowgirl

position so she was facing him. Jack took the opportunity to play with her big titties. He squeezed them like melons, fondled the nipples, then took turns taking each aroused nipple into his mouth. All the while his wife rocked back and forth on his member, grinding it deep into her cunt and stimulating her clitoris at the same time.

"These two are like professional fuckers," one man stated.

A girl responded, "They are, stupid."

Jamelia went to town on Jack's dick now, utilizing all nine inches as she constantly impaled herself upon it. She was screaming with pleasure, her eyes squeezed shut, her face a picture of pleasure and immense concentration. Jack knew she was building for an earth-shattering climax and was about to erupt.

When she came she tilted her head skyward and howled at the sun a moment before some cloud cover obscured it. Juice flooded her cunt and squirted from her slit. Jack felt the spray follow a line right up to his chest and some even managed to reach his chin. Jamelia kept going, making certain to extract every ounce of pleasure from her climax that she could. It went on for at least a minute before she finally relaxed and slumped exhausted on top of Jack.

"That took...a lot...out of me," she panted.

"If you're too tired to make him come, I'll do it," the young woman with the wet pussy eagerly volunteered.

Jamelia looked at Jack and he nodded his consent. Jamelia

got off her husband and sat in the sand while the girl knelt beside Jack's cock and took it into her hand.

Jack lay there and relaxed as the girl jerked him off. She was pretty adept at it and he knew she would have no trouble making him come quite quickly.

Everyone watched on with unblinking anticipation, waiting for their friend to make the star ejaculate. Jack could feel the first faint sensations of climax starting to form down below. Very soon the cum swirled in his balls and the tingles increased rapidly. Jizz surged up his shaft and shot from the head of his cock. Jack grunted loudly with each squirt and his climax was greeted with claps and cheers from the onlookers. By the time he was done a sea of cum covered his body. The girl who'd successfully wanked him off smiled at the mess with satisfaction and got back to her feet.

The crowd left soon after and the two sexually satisfied porn stars went back into the surf for another swim.

In the Flesh

T oday was the big day.

Will and Carla had now known each other for two months. The only thing was, they'd never actually met in the flesh. So far it had been a long distance relationship with interaction solely via webcam chat and telephone conversations. The pair had actually got in touch through a mutual Facebook friend who thought they might be perfect for one another.

Carla was gorgeous and Will couldn't believe his luck. But more than that, she seemed even more beautiful on the inside than she was on the outside. In cyber world they were getting along great. One never could really tell, though, until they actually met in person.

Will was feeling edgy and nervous, so he took his morning coffee outside so he could smoke a cigarette. Carla didn't smoke, but was aware that Will did. She assured him she was okay with it, so long as he didn't smoke indoors or in the car. He never did anyway.

She was flying in from interstate this afternoon to meet him. Will lit a cigarette and ran scenarios through his head as he smoked and sipped his coffee. What would she be like in person? Would they hit it off just as well in real life as they did over the net and the phone? After two months of chatting, would they have anything to say to one another when finally talking face to face?

He shrugged and stabbed out his smoke. Too much analysis. The answers to those questions would have to wait until later that day, when she stepped off that plane and he held her in his waiting arms for the very first time.

It was a Saturday, a day off work. Time crawled slowly like a dying dog. Will repeatedly checked his watch, willing two o'clock to come round, indicating it was time to head out to the airport. He kept himself occupied by doing chores. The lawn got mowed and the edges trimmed. The gardens were weeded and the house vacuumed. He'd already thoroughly cleaned the kitchen and bathrooms the night before, so they didn't really need doing other than a last minute touch up. To finish off he made sure everything was basically neat and tidy. By the time he was done his watch was just shy of midday.

"Man, this has been the longest morning of my life," he complained to himself.

Outside he smoked another cigarette and spent a moment admiring his lawn and gardens. He wished he had a pool. Maybe one day he would get one put in. There was certainly room for a pool and some surrounding decking. Definitely worth considering.

By the time he'd had some lunch, showered, shaved and changed into some fresh clothes, it was finally time to go. Nerves mounting by the second, Will started the car and backed out of the garage, then headed off in the direction of the airport.

The afternoon was clear and warm without being hot. It was perfect, actually. Will had the windows down to let through some breeze, enjoying the feel of it on his face. Traffic was fairly heavy until he got to the outskirts of town. Once on the motorway he made good time to the airport and arrived twenty minutes before Carla's flight was due to land. He parked the car and stood outside the terminal building, having another smoke before going inside. He made his way to the arrivals lounge and took a seat, idly watching a quiz show on a TV screen overhead. He found he couldn't sit still and mentally tried to pacify himself. He didn't want to be edgy when they met. He wanted to at least appear calm and relaxed.

As it turned out the flight was delayed by fifteen minutes. Not exactly helping Will to chill and relax. As the passengers started to file into the arrivals lounge, Will's heart pumped hard in his chest. He took a deep breath and let it out slowly, temporarily holding it when he set eyes on Carla. She spied him in the crowd and rushed over, wrapping her arms tightly around his neck. She smelled of sweet perfume. Which brand he couldn't determine, but he didn't care. She smelled great.

"It's so good to finally meet you and touch you," she gushed.

Will held her at arm's length and smiled, taking in her beauty. Her dark hair flowed over slender shoulders and came to rest just above her enticing cleavage. She wore a summery yellow dress with a flower pattern that hugged her curves

189

casually, but exquisitely. He leaned in and kissed her lightly on the lips. The kiss lingered without getting passionate.

"We should go get your bag," he suggested.

"Good idea."

Fifteen minutes later they were driving back towards the city and Will's home. While they drove they chatted lightly, the conversation flowing easily, which was a good sign and a relief for Will. They definitely hadn't run out of things to say to one another. He pulled into the garage and used the remote to close the door behind the car. Carrying Carla's bag into the house, he offered her a seat on the couch and went into the kitchen to make tea.

"Sure you wouldn't like something stronger?" he called out as he put the kettle on.

"Not right now. Maybe later."

A few minutes later and Will went back to the living room carrying a tray with two cups of tea and a small plate of shortbread biscuits. He placed the tray on the coffee table and sat down beside Carla, encroaching on her personal space without actually touching her. She offered him a smile that still held a hint of nervousness. If he was honest, although he was way more relaxed than he had been most of the day, he was still a little nervous as well. It would pass.

That evening Will took Carla to a local Thai restaurant which was just a few blocks down the road. The sun was setting when they arrived and it was full dark by the time they left. Arm in arm and tipsy from a few wines, they strolled the short distance back to Will's house. Carla enjoyed the clear, quiet night, constantly gazing up at the stars as they walked.

By the time they arrived home, Will was in the mood for another drink, and he immediately went to the kitchen and cracked open a bottle of chilled white wine. He poured two generous glasses and took them into the living room where Carla was relaxed on the couch, high heel shoes off, waiting for him. He handed her a glass and she kissed him on the lips as a gesture of gratitude. She tasted the wine and nodded.

"Nice," she said with approval.

Will was half tempted to duck outside and smoke a cigarette with his wine, but he refrained. He sensed Carla might be open to some affection and possibly some loving, so he decided to stay put. Instead, he moved in closer until the sides of their bodies were touching. She didn't seem to mind. In fact, he felt she was quite happy for him to be as close to her as he so desired.

They finished the glasses of wine and Carla excused herself to go to the bathroom. Will relaxed on the lounge, feeling quite chilled now after spending more face time with her and consuming some alcohol. When she returned she surprised him by sitting on his lap, wrapping her slender arms around his neck and clamping her mouth firmly upon his. Their lips parted and wet tongues met in a sensual and stimulating embrace.

Will immediately felt his cock stir inside his pants. It

stiffened and strained against the clothing in a desperate bid to get out. He placed a hand on her bare thigh and chanced inching it under her dress until his fingertips were touching the hem of her lacy panties. For the moment her legs were crossed, but as his hand probed lower in search of her honeypot, she opened her legs for him and placed a foot on the floor. Will now had access to her cunt, and when he touched it through the flimsy material of her underwear, he discovered her pussy was on fire, with juice already seeping through the fabric.

Carla broke the kiss and groaned as he applied pressure to her burning snatch. "Slip a finger inside me," she whispered and thrust her tongue deep into his mouth once more.

Will slid a finger beneath the material and it sank into her wet spot immediately, hot juice marinating the digit. He thrust it in and out of her, applied pressure to the spongy walls of her interior, causing little squeals of pleasure to escape her throat as she kissed him. His hard on was digging into the flesh under her right thigh. She searched it out with her left hand and massaged his erection through his pants. Suddenly she broke into a smile and pulled her face away from his.

"In all our conversations," she said, "you never once hinted that you were so well-endowed."

Will shrugged. "I didn't want to brag."

She kept rubbing him. "That feels very impressive." She got off him then and knelt on the carpet, her hands busy undoing his belt and then his zipper. "I need to take a look at this." Carla slid his pants and underwear down his thighs, then held his throbbing cock upright and studied it with excited eyes. "I'm a very lucky girl." She licked her lips and continued to eye his member with hunger and intense lust.

Will kicked off his shoes and socks and, with Carla's help, got free of his pants and underwear. She started licking his cock from base to tip and he climbed out of his shirt and tossed it away onto the floor. He then reclined on the lounge and watched with great interest as Carla's lips and tongue pleasured his pole. She ran circles around his balls, then sucked one gently into her mouth. Her tongue was then on the move again, tracing a line up his long length, where she now ran wet circles around the head of his cock.

"Suck it," he urged her, desperate to feel it sliding deep down her throat.

She grinned cheekily, her blue eyes staring into his. "Patience," she crooned and continued to tease him with light licks and nips with her pouting lips. "This is worth savoring," she added.

Will closed his eyes and just enjoyed the tingles of pleasure she was inflicting upon him. Still she teased, returning to his balls and tasting them once more. He felt her tongue go back up his cock and he willed her to finally take it into her mouth. This time she did and sucked eagerly on the head, causing ripples of intense tingles to surge all through his body.

"That's it," he said. "That's what I want."

Carla giggled and continued to suck hard on his dick. She worked her mouth further down his shaft until she'd swallowed half of it, then she let it slide back out of her mouth until only the head was still inside. Will placed a hand on the back of her head and thrust into her mouth as one of her hands stroked the stem.

Inch by inch she took his length down her throat until the head of his dick was probing her tonsils. Still she continued to swallow him until her bottom lip was kissing his balls. He had an eight inch dick so her effort was quite impressive.

"That feels so good," Will said as Carla slowly let his cock slide back out of her mouth. It sprang free of her lips and hit his lower abs with a solid thud of flesh on flesh.

Another grin from Carla. "Will you return the favor?"

Will leaped from the couch and quickly helped her undress until she was starkers. Carla then sat back and got comfortable, spreading her legs wide apart and exposing a glorious pussy that was waxed silken smooth. Will couldn't wait to get into it and literally dove between her thighs and latched onto her waiting cunt.

Carla was unbelievably juiced up, her soft lips wet and slippery. His keen tongue sank deep into her soaking passage and he used his lips to suck warm, sweet, tantalizing pussy juice into his mouth.

Yum! he thought as he devoured her delicious little cunt.

"Suck my clit," she directed. "I like that. My clit is really sensitive."

Will kissed his way up to her throbbing clitoris and nibbled it between his lips. Carla flinched and sighed with pleasure. He thrashed the small, hard node with his tongue, then sucked it hard. All the while she squirmed around on the lounge, uttering incoherent words of ecstasy amid a symphony of moans and groans and incessant panting. By the time his mouth returned to the opening to her tunnel, he found a fresh river of juice had flooded her horny cunt.

Feeding on her like a starving man, Will thought for sure he would soon bring her to a dramatic climax. However, that never happened, despite his efforts to give her one. Eventually he came up for air, his face glistening with her feminine moisture.

"I was trying to make you come," he told her.

He must have looked disappointed, because she replied, "Don't worry about it. As much as I love a man going down on me, I've never been able to come that way." She smiled. "I'll come when you fuck me, Baby."

Will took that as an invitation to slip a length into her, so he positioned himself between her legs and guided his cock into her hole, where he managed to bury himself all the way inside her with one long and very deep thrust.

They both groaned in unison when the head of his thick dick rammed the end of her passage. She was so fucking hot and wet inside. The sensation against the sensitive skin of his prick was incredible. It had been a while since he'd had a girlfriend;

especially one he liked and desired as much as Carla. Apart from getting his own sexual satisfaction, he really wanted to please her.

"Stroke me slow and deep this way and you'll have me coming in no time," she let him know.

Will ran his hands tenderly over her pert and lovely breasts as his penis stroked into her rhythmically. His balls were very full and swung heavily in their sack. They slapped against the cheeks of her ass each and every time he penetrated her fully. Her pussy was making wet, kissing noises as he fucked it, as if her cunt were trying to suck on his cock.

"Your pussy feels fantastic," he told her, eyes roaming all over her naked flesh. "You have such a nice body. The photos you sent me all looked great, but you look even sexier in person."

"Thank you, lover."

Will fell silent and just concentrated on bringing his woman to her first ever orgasm with him. His hands were now clasping her thighs as he humped her just a little bit faster. Carla had her eyes closed, lips parted, constant panting escaping from them. Every so often her tongue would dart out and flick seductively over those lips, painting them with a wet sheen that rendered them oh so sumptuous.

Five minutes later her body really started to tense up. Her pants had progressed to deep and urgent moans. She started wriggling around rather restlessly on the couch, almost as if trying to move away from his thudding cock. Will gripped her legs tighter and rammed her harder until their bodies were smacking together. His cock throbbed deep inside her cunt, the thickness of it stretching her lips wide apart.

She suddenly announced, "I'm getting really close."

Will increased the tempo, thumping his shaft into her with more aggression. He wanted her to explode all over his cock and that's exactly what she did. Her pussy erupted like a volcano, hot lava juice flooding her passage while her body convulsed in the climactic throes of orgasm.

When she was done and her body started to relax, Will pulled out of her, feeling totally rapt that he'd just brought her to her very first orgasm with him. It was a small milestone, but one that pleased him immensely.

"That was mind-blowing," she said with a satisfied grin. "You have an awesome cock, Will, and you really know how to use it."

He nodded a thank you and returned her smile a little sheepishly.

Without either of them saying a word, Will swapped places with her and Carla prepared to mount him. Before she did she took his wet dick into her mouth once more and happily sampled her own flavor from it before straddling him and inserting it back into her horny little pussy.

God she was tight, Will mused as he watched her bounce up and down on top of him. Within seconds his balls were wet with her juices and her pussy made sucking noises as she fucked him. He played with her beautiful titties and ground against her crotch from beneath, helping to drive his full length inside her and stimulate the very end of her canal.

"Fuck it," he told her.

She responded with, "I am."

"Fuck it harder. Make yourself come all over my cock again."

She grinned at him. "Maybe I don't want to."

"You do."

Carla placed one hand on his shoulder and reached behind her with the other, where she used her fingers to stroke up and down his shaft as she rode his cock.

"You've got me so wet, Babe," she said.

"Good. I want you to get wet over me."

"No problems there."

"We've definitely got sexual chemistry happening."

"We certainly have," she readily agreed.

Carla concentrated on fucking her man while still feeling his cock with her hand. Will entertained himself with her boobs, watching them bob up and down on her chest and occasionally playing with them.

"Gorgeous," he whispered hoarsely.

"What?"

"I said you're gorgeous."

Carla thudded down on him, his words of praise encouraging

her to really fuck him hard. Her pussy squelched as her cunt lips suctioned up and down his length, filling herself gleefully with his hot throbbing meat. His balls swirled around in their sack, preparing a healthy load of fresh cum for tonight's thrilling conclusion. He had a lot to give her, built up through months of abstinence, and he couldn't wait to unload inside her, or wherever she wished him to deposit his serve of semen.

But that would come later.

"I'm getting really close again," she said. "Fuck!"

"Do it. Come on me."

Will slapped both cheeks of her ass hard, spurring her on, encouraging her to fuck him and come on his dick. To help her out he placed his hands flat on the lounge and lunged into her from below, driving his length into her soaking depths and bringing squeals of intense pleasure from her lips.

"My...God!" Carla screamed as her body went into a series of convulsions. Her flesh shivered and quivered as the severity of the orgasm rocked her world. "It's...so...fucking...awesome!"

Will continued to slam into her, his flesh smacking against hers. His breath came in short, sharp bursts. Adrenalin pumped through his veins, increasing the effects of the hormones in his bloodstream. He slapped her ass again and gave two final, powerful thrusts that stretched the very end of her cunt tunnel. Carla suddenly went limp as if shot and fell forward into his arms. There she rested, breathing short and ragged breaths, a light sheen of perspiration covering her face and upper body.

Will felt doubly satisfied now. He'd made her come twice.

After a few sips of wine, Will positioned her on all fours down on the carpet and immediately entered her from the rear. He varied the pace and depth of his strokes, sometimes barely nudging the head of his cock inside her pussy before driving it hard to the very end and grinding it into her.

She said, "You've got me so turned on, Babe."

"You and me both. My cock feels so hard. That's your fault."

She giggled and moaned at the same time. "I'm happy to take the blame for that."

Will watched his dick disappearing inside his lover. She had such a beautiful little pussy. His cock glistened with her ample coating of juice and his balls were soaked with it from when she was on top. Carla reached a hand between his legs, searched out his dangling testicles and played with them with her fingertips.

"That feels really nice," he told her, encouraging her to keep doing that.

"Is this all for me?" she asked, indicating the cum in his sack. "I want us to come at the same time. Do you think you can make that happen?"

"I'll give it my best shot," Will said with a grin. "Just let me know when you're getting close."

"Okay."

"Do you want me to come inside you?"

"Of course. I'm dying to feel you squirt in me."

They both concentrated on reaching a simultaneous climax.

Will stroked her deeply and rhythmically, just like he had done when doing her missionary.

"I'm getting closer," she announced. "Keep going...just like you are."

He now focused on himself and soon felt the tingles of release starting to build in his genitals. Carla's panting became more urgent as her tension built and Will wasn't sure he was going to last long enough.

His fears were allayed when his very first burst of cum shot deep into her pussy and sparked the first wave of her orgasm. She came and he came. His dick's load flooded her cunt where it mingled with a fresh sea of Carla juice. When they were both spent they flopped sideways onto the carpet where Will cuddled her from behind, his cock still trapped within her cunt.

They lay there catching their breath and just basking in the wonderful afterglow of their very first time together.

"That was so nice," Carla said softly. "I'm so glad we're finally together in the flesh." She giggled. "Literally."

"It's been a hell of a first meeting, even better than I'd hoped for."

Carla eased herself away from him and turned around to face him. She kissed him firmly on the lips several times. "So," she said, propping herself up on an elbow. "Are you coming down to visit me next weekend?"

Also in the series:

Printed in Great Britain
by Amazon

74538696R00115